50¢ ⁵⁵

DATE DUE

DEC 1 JR '80			
GAYLORD			

The Running of the Deer

THE
RUNNING
OF THE
DEER

Ewan Clarkson

Drawings by David Stone

E. P. DUTTON & CO., INC. • NEW YORK • 1972

Library of Congress Catalog Card Number: 71-179849
SBN: 0-525-19473-8

43,508

To the memory of my father

The Running of the Deer

1

The Calves of Summer

His name was Rhus, and he came with the dawn, to lie sprawled and shivering on the short, dew-drenched turf of the combe.

His mother had chosen well. The previous evening, as the nightjar called and the white owl drifted along the hedge by Dunkery Gate, she had made her way, slowly and alone, to this narrow valley. She had kept below the shoulders of the hills, so that her outline did not show against the night sky, for the wild red deer of Exmoor had long ago learned that survival in such close proximity to man depended largely on stealth.

The combe she had chosen was little more than a

crack or fissure in the smoothly rounded slopes of the high moor. Here, amid a tangle of fern, scrub oak, and spindly birch, she had rested during the remainder of the short, scented night, patiently keeping vigil until the stars began to pale, and a faint aura of light glowed over the eastern hills.

Now, still trembling with the shock of the birth, she began to groom her calf, licking him with rough care. In a few moments he was able to sit up, his head swaying and weaving on his long neck, and soon he was standing, his spindly legs well splayed out. He took a few tottering steps, fell, and stood up again, this time with more confidence, and his tail wagged as he breathed the morning air.

His mother watched nervously. Already the day was astir. A blackbird sang in the rowan tree as light flooded the moor and far away could be heard the lowing of cattle as they waited to make their slow way to the milking parlor. Now the hind was anxious to take cover, to conceal herself during the long hours of daylight. Gently she nudged her calf, guiding him to the edge of the little clearing.

Here she pushed him down on to a soft bed of dry grass and fern. He lay where he fell, and watched with dark eyes as his mother walked away, to vanish from sight in the undergrowth.

Rhus lay still, and so well did he blend with his surroundings that he was all but invisible. The silky hair on his flanks was the red of the dead fern, while the heavy dappling of cream spots that overlaid his background color matched the sere yellow of the grass and the light of the sun as it filtered through the birch leaves. Tall green fern broke his outline and shaded his face. Only his eyes, round and dark in the dome of his high forehead, betrayed him.

At this stage of his life he was completely trusting, utterly devoid of fear. So he felt no anxiety at the departure of his mother. He was also without desire. He knew no hunger or thirst, felt no need to wander, so he simply stayed where he was put. He felt the sun warm on his back, and he slept a little, weary after the exertions of his birth.

His mother slept too, but it was the sleep of her kind, a momentary loss of consciousness, from which she could recover in an instant, wide awake and ready at once for any emergency. The slightest sound, or the faintest whiff of danger, was all she needed to rouse her.

Rhus did not know it, but she was only twenty yards away from him. After she had left him, she had cleansed herself of the afterbirth and made her way to the tiny stream that formed the bed of the combe. Here, in a rocky pool where small trout flickered and darted like shadows, she had drunk deep, before bathing in the cold, clear water. Only then did she take up her station close to her calf.

All the long day she stood on guard. She heard the raven as he sailed the sky on stretched, stiff-pinioned wings. She saw the buzzard as he wheeled high and circled overhead. Both birds saw Rhus, but they also noted the presence of the hind. So they passed by, having no wish to face her anger or the slashing of her hooves.

11

The greatest danger the hind feared was attack from marauding farm dogs. Many of these were large and half-wild, accustomed to dealing with cattle and sheep. The dogs well knew when the deer were calving and often hunted in pairs, or even small packs. Against such killers the hind could not hope to protect her calf and was in some danger herself. Fortunately, the moors were wide and high, and the dogs lived on farms in the valleys, so the chance of Rhus's being discovered by these predators was fairly remote.

The long day drifted by. It was very hot in the combe. Summer had come to the shores of the Severn sea, and the air was heavy with the spice of growth. Perfume of gorse and rowan blossom, scent of fern and grass and water-wet stone, above all the rich tang of moist, fermenting earth, all were mixed and blended by the breeze that blew soft and warm from the south.

Already the flies had found Rhus, the flies that were to plague him every summer of his life. They settled round his eyes, avid for moisture. They tickled his nostrils and lips and crawled on his skin in shiny black hordes. From time to time Rhus shook his head and twitched his hide in an effort to be rid of them, and then they would rise in a buzzing cloud. Yet always they returned, persevering, patient, impersonal. Only the stupefying cold of night overcame them.

Not until dusk dropped a purple cloak over the moor did the hind emerge from the fern. Even then she did not go straight to her calf, but stood still, waiting and listening until she was sure all was well. Satisfied, she then approached Rhus and blew softly on his head.

14

Rhus stood up and stretched. His legs felt stronger, surer, and he took a few dancing steps. The milky, musky scent of his mother beckoned him, and he soon discovered where the smell of milk was strongest. Eagerly he muzzled into her flank, craving the rich moisture he knew was there, if only he could discover how to obtain it.

His first attempts to suckle were disastrous. His mother's milk flowed freely—too freely, for he had yet to master the art of swallowing, and he sputtered and sneezed, totally unprepared for the warm stream that gushed into his mouth.

He tried again, this time with more caution, and with better success. His mother stood patiently, and soon he was feeding lustily, until he was full.

The hind began to feed now, moving slowly up the side of the combe as she browsed. Her diet was varied. She cropped the young growing shoots of the brambles, nipping the tips where the thorns had not yet toughened. She found a patch of sweet grass which the sheep had missed, and ripped a curling tendril of ivy from the stem of a gorse bush. She bit the succulent sprouting stems of young ash, and tore the new growth of heather and whortleberry. It was the time of rich feeding, and she could afford to be selective in her diet, taking only the best the countryside could provide, to nourish herself and her calf.

Rhus stayed by her side, sniffing the air and listening to the tiny sounds that punctuated the dark pages of the night. From time to time he lay down, but only for short periods. Hourly he grew stronger, more eager to explore his new world, but his mother kept a wary eye on him as she fed, and did not let him stray far from her side. So the short night passed, and dawn came bringing with it a cold mist, which blanketed the valleys and lay like white cotton wool in the combe. Rhus lay above the mist, above the tree line, with only the tall fern for shelter. Here the air was cooler and the flies less troublesome, and here his mother left him for yet another day.

A week went by, and still Rhus knew nothing of his domain save the close confines of the combe. At the time of his birth, he had weighed little more than twelve pounds, but he gained weight rapidly. His hooves, which had been pearly white, had darkened, and their ragged edges had worn clean and smooth from contact with the ground. Although his legs were still absurdly long and spindly, they were much stronger, so that now he could easily outrun a man. He no longer spent his days alone on a bed of fern, but stayed by his mother's side.

He still wore his baby coat of russet, heavily dappled with cream, and here he was in sharp contrast to his mother. She had not yet shed her winter coat, and her hair was dull brown, fading almost to yellow. Loose tufts of fur clung to the sides of her cheeks, giving her a quaint appearance as if she sported muttonchop whiskers. She was gaunt and lean, having nurtured her calf through the rigors of winter and spring. Now she had to provide milk for him, and so she fed ravenously, by day as well as by night.

The weather stayed hot and dry, and the new growth,

which a month ago had thrust so urgently from the soil, slackened as each plant and shrub, fern and tree, harbored its resources, concentrating on root growth in its search for moisture. On the seventh evening of his life, the hind led Rhus out of the combe, and up onto the high moor.

Here the air was colder, and Rhus shivered in the wind that blew from the sea. His mother moved purposefully over the short, wiry heather, following the trails which, though scarcely discernible amid the tough vegetation, had been known and followed by her kind for centuries. Rhus followed by the wan light of the stars. A flock of sheep looked up inquiringly as they passed, and a pony snorted and shied as they woke him from a doze. Once a big bird flew up from under their hooves with a battering whir of wings. It was a black-cock, one of the few surviving members of his kind on the moor.

Now for a long way the trail led downhill, and the heather grew deeper and more luxuriant, giving way to fern and tall grass. They came at last to another combe, similiar to the one they had left, but wider and less precipitous. Here, in a small glade beside the stream, familiar dark forms grazed, a group of hinds which raised their heads in greeting.

Rhus stood meekly at his mother's side. Two of the hinds had calves at foot, and one had a yearling calf as well. The third hind was old and rangy, and she had no calf. She was the leader of the herd, and Rhus's mother knew her well. In fact, she was the old hind's granddaughter, although neither of them realized the fact. As a calf the old hind had been attacked by a fox, which had bitten off half her right ear before being driven away by the drumming hooves of her mother. That had been eleven years ago, and still she survived, respected and venerated by all the younger deer.

She was one of the matriarchs of a mighty tribe, the proud race of red deer that had inhabited England since before the Ice Age. Exmoor was their last great stronghold, a crumbling ruin which each year grew a little smaller. Because of its beauty and the wild grandeur of its scenery, the area had been declared a national park, but although the park covered more than two hundred and fifty square miles, from the wild wooded cliffs that bordered the Severn sea in the north, over the high moors to the gentle lowlands in the south, only a small portion was uncultivated.

Out of a total of one hundred and seventy thousand acres, only fifty thousand acres were wild moorland. Even this remnant was scattered, broken and intersected by roads and villages, isolated copses and farms. Each year men took and tamed another small area of moor, five acres here, or ten there. This land they fenced and ploughed, spreading lime and sowing grass as keep for their sheep and cattle. In addition they used the high moors, turning their sheep and ponies out to graze.

The red deer knew no frontiers. They recognized no barriers, natural or artificial, and they drew no distinction between wild land and tame. They lived with men, and among men, and although they feared mankind, they paid little heed to him. Where necessary, they hid by day and fed by night, and came and went between arable land and the moors much as they pleased.

So it came about that as soon as the calves were old enough, Half Ear led her small band down off the moor, into the valley, where small fields surrounded by high beech hedges were rich with sweet green grass. Here the hinds fed greedily, pulling at the lush fodder and swallowing it whole. Half Ear ate more sparingly, getting her fill, but keeping careful watch, and listening intently for any sound that might spell danger.

As soon as the hinds had finished eating and were beginning to lie down to chew the cud, Half Ear led them away, back to the safety of the moor. Ever cautious, she always waited for night to fall before she moved off the moor, and she was ever careful to return well before dawn.

For Rhus, life in that first short summer was uneventful. He spent the long hot days dozing in the sun, or romping with the other calves among the hinds. At night he followed his mother as she accompanied the rest of the herd. She had grown sleek and fat, shedding her bleached and faded coat and emerging resplendent in her new robe of red. Always there was plenty of milk for Rhus, and in addition he had begun to sample whatever his mother ate. He had no need of the food, but he enjoyed the savor, the strange new sensations on his palate. He was the first of the calves to lose his dappled spots, and by the middle of August he was in the true red livery of his kind.

In company with the rest of the herd, he felt a great bond of affection for Half Ear. One member or another would be constantly at her side, grooming her coat with their long thick tongues. Half Ear liked this, and would stand for hours in drowsy contentment, her head hung low and her eyes closed. As a result of this attention her hide was particularly glossy and luxuriant.

One night strangers came to the combe. Their hides were black in the moonlight, and their antlers glowed bone white. One stag was massive, stout barreled and thick of neck, his antlers tall and branched in a wide arc above his head. The other stag was smaller, his antlers less developed.

Stags and hinds regarded one another with mild interest for a few moments, and then the stags passed by. They were on their way to raid the ripe grain. The fever of the rut had not yet come upon them.

2

The Rut

Autumn came in a spatter of rain, and the wind piled the beech leaves into golden drifts against the hedges. Frost bronzed the bracken fern, and the rowan berries were red against the sky. Half Ear led her band out of the combe, north over the moor to the oak woods by the Severn sea. The woods stretched as far as the eye could follow, rolling in dark majesty, clothing the bare bones of the land.

The oaks were the great providers. Their roots spread far, binding the substance of the hills, trapping the vast water resources and mining the salts and minerals, efficiently, frugally, wasting nothing. In the summer their leaves spread a canopy of shade over the land, so that the soil remained moist and cool. When gales blew, bringing rain lashing from the Atlantic, the trees bore the brunt of the shock, and the rain, instead of cutting spitefully into the earth, was lowered gently to the ground.

In winter the trees stood bare, but their leaves, lying in a thick russet carpet, still shielded the earth, slowly disintegrating and decaying, releasing their wealth back into the soil, a blanket against rain and frost, a rich storehouse of insect food for the birds that scratched the forest floor.

Each spring hosts of caterpillars hatched from eggs that had overwintered in crevices among the rough bark, and the grubs fell among the young leaves as they emerged, yellow and tender, from their tight bud cases. At times the numbers of grubs were so vast, their appetites so huge, that they threatened to defoliate the oaks and, in so doing, destroy themselves. Birds came, flocking from afar, to depopulate the armies of caterpillars, and the ground beneath the oaks was white with their droppings, each tiny offering a significant contribution to the economy of the forest.

The oaks, it seemed, were immortal. Only injury or disease could lay them low. Even in death, long after the branches had crumbled, the decaying trunks played host to a rich variety of life, both animal and vegetable. Mosses grew on the sodden bark, ferns sprouted in the debris-filled hollows and fungi flung up their garish citadels, only to vanish as swiftly as they had come.

Insects bored and tunneled through the soft outer wood, and in the hidden galleries their grubs grew fat.

Wasps came and took paper for their nests. Slowworms, toads, frogs, and newts sheltered beneath the log, and in the spring a sleepy adder lay coiled in the sunshine. Death and slow decay was imperative to life.

The greatest benison of the oaks came each autumn, as the acorns swelled and ripened in their cups. They fell like rain when a breeze stirred the treetops, spattering down on to the forest floor, long before the leaves had faded and died. Throughout the autumn they continued to fall, to be buried by the withered leaves that followed.

Yet of the countless tons of fruit that lay scattered on the forest floor, only a tiny proportion survived to reach germination, and those were mostly planted by jays who, having eaten as many acorns as their crops would hold, carried others away in their beaks and planted them deep in the turf. Even then, few oaks grew, for as soon as the growing plant showed above the earth it was cropped short, eaten by rabbit or hare, sheep or deer or forest pony.

The rest of the oak harvest was eaten as soon as it fell from the oak, the creatures of the wild flocking to the feast. It was to this banquet that Half Ear led her band, and the hinds stuffed themselves on the hard, bitter fruit.

The woods were full of deer, as herds from all over the moor converged to share the spoil. During the day the deer moved away uphill, up to where the trees were shrunken and wind shriven, and the gorse and fern grew thick. Here they hid from the humans that used the woods, late holidaymakers who explored the running streams and followed the twisting pathways. Even when the last of the holidaymakers had gone, the woods were still crowded with people each weekend, as long as the weather remained fine, but few saw the deer.

The deer largely ignored the humans. They stood high on the hills and watched as men and women passed by. If anyone came too close they moved away, quietly and without haste, easily outdistancing the intruders. Few humans looked up, and those that did failed to notice the herds among the trees.

Each evening, as dusk gathered over the land, Half Ear led the hinds down out of the trees, first to drink at the stream and then to feed on the acorns. One favorite spot lay on the broad floor of the valley, above a small birch grove that bordered a spring. The spring formed a swampy hollow, and here the ground was pitted by the slots of countless hoofprints, where the deer had bathed and wallowed in the muddy water.

One evening in late September, Rhus fed with the herd above the spring. It was quite dark, for the sun had long since set, and the waning moon had still not climbed above the hill. Half Ear, who had been feeding as busily as the rest, raised her head with a jerk, listening.

The sound came again, high on the hill, a dry tapping, faint but clear, as if someone was knocking the branches with a stick. The noise came nearer, moving slowly down the valley, and then came the call, a deep bellowing roar that echoed among the oaks and died away in a gurgling growl. The hinds waited, food forgotten as their whole being responded to the familiar call.

As the moon topped the trees the stag appeared, his eyes glaring white, his shaggy neck swollen and his whole body shaking with the fever of the rut. Ignoring the hinds, he knelt at the spring, thrusting his chin and neck into the mud. Swinging his head, he showered himself with a great wave of water and slime, and then sprawled full length, wallowing from side to side in an effort to quench the torment that burned inside him.

Suddenly he leapt to his feet and, in an explosion of blind savagery, attacked a small tree that grew by the spring. His great antlers clattered against the spindly trunk, sending twigs and strips of bark flying, and the tree rocked as he strove to tear it up by the roots.

His anger cooled as swiftly as it had flamed and, as if remembering the hinds, he turned toward them. Rhus and the other calves bunched together in fear, a little distance away from the hinds, who watched, motionless, as the stag slowly drew near.

From the shadows by the stream another stag called, belling deep down and grunting angrily as it crashed through the undergrowth. The first stag stopped dead, and as his rival approached he turned, rolling his eyes, his head weaving as he displayed the whole length of his massive body. Then, with a grunt, he charged.

The two stags met head on, with a splintering crash that echoed through the hills. Antlers locked, necks bulging, they wrestled and strained, their hind legs stiff and stretched as each tried to throw the other off balance, to thrust the other's head aside for the split second each needed to drive home the terrible brow points that could pierce hide and rib, to tear at liver, lungs, or heart.

For a moment it seemed that the first stag would be defeated, as slowly, step by step, his rival forced him to yield ground. Then suddenly, with a burst of power that sent mud and turf flying, he sent the challenger flying backward at such a speed that he rolled him over.

The battle was won, and without waiting for further punishment the intruding stag turned and fled, but not before receiving a resounding blow on his hindquarters. The victor roared his triumph and scored the ground with his antlers, sending grass, twigs, and fern showering over his mud-stained shoulders. Then he turned, and trotted purposefully toward the waiting hinds.

The stag stayed with the hinds for three weeks, following the herd wherever it went, and during that time he shared his favors among each of the hinds, all except Half Ear. His bizarre appearance, his rolling, tormented eyes, mud-stained flanks, and swollen, shaggy neck, together with his pronounced smell and wild behavior, excited and stimulated the hinds, arousing them to full fertility. Half Ear remained aloof and unaffected.

Each courtship was as sudden and shocking as one of his rages, an assault so violent as to be almost an attack. Throughout this period he ate and slept little, pacing restlessly round his herd and guarding them from the attentions of other stags. Challengers were frequent, especially the younger stags, who were constantly on the watch for a chance at a few moments' dalliance with one of the hinds. At first they were quickly routed, and once the older stag won three more hinds from another stag, sending him limping away with a gaping tear in his shoulder.

At first it seemed that nothing would staunch the flow of his energy and explosive vitality, but as the weeks passed the fires of his own passions consumed his strength. He began to slow down, to conserve his energy. No longer did he wreck an anthill in mindless fury, or thrash the branches of a holly tree until the berries flew in a shower of bright red rain. He lost weight, and his bellowing roars were heard less frequently.

He met his defeat in the gray light of a drizzling dawn, as the herd made its way uphill out of the wood. He had just fought, and beaten after a long hard struggle, a young and heavy stag, when he was attacked by yet another. The ground was steeply sloping, and his attacker had the advantage of high ground. The old warrior met the charge gamely, but he had neither the strength nor the stomach for battle. In a few moments he found himself slipping and sliding downhill, retreating rapidly to avoid being impaled on the other's brow points. Suddenly he broke away and fled, leaving the victor shaking his head and grunting angrily after him before trotting away uphill to claim his harem.

His was a hollow victory. Most of the hinds had already conceived and were indifferent to him. He lost the herd that same day to another rival, and this was the pattern all over the moor as the older stags relinquished their holds over the hinds, and the younger stags took over. The first white fires of the rut had died, and only the glowing embers sputtered and sparked.

Slowly the weather deteriorated, as the nights grew colder, and the days shorter. When the weather was calm the moors lay shrouded in a gray mist. Moisture was everywhere, glistening on the tree trunks, staining the bare rocks, sparkling like shattered crystal on fern and leaf and twig. The air was cold and dank, redolent with rot and decay, with fungoid growth and moldering bark.

When the wind blew, the clouds fell as rain, swelling the great sponges of the bogs and filling the streams that foamed and chattered over the rocks. The sun, when it shone, was pale and white, hanging low over the hills and shedding a weak light that was without warmth or power.

As the leaves left the oaks the wood pigeons came, great flocks of greedy gray birds in search of the acorns that remained on the forest floor. Each dawn heard the clatter of their wings, and each night their numbers darkened the sky as, with crops crammed to bursting, they flew heavily away to roost.

The deer were impervious to the weather. Their coats grew thicker, the color fading from a rich red to a drab gray brown. Still led by Half Ear, the herd lingered on in the woods, together with the three hinds that had joined them during the rut. Rhus was growing fast. Although he still fed from his mother, he had little need of her milk and could have survived quite well on his own.

Food and feeding preoccupied the entire herd at this time. As yet the forest continued to spread a rich repast for the deer. Acorns were still to be found, hidden in mossy crevices among the rocks and buried beneath the leaves. In the lower hollows of the woods were groves of young ash, hazel, and birch trees. The deer browsed on the leafless shoots, biting them back until the wood grew too thick and hard. In the spring, the trees would put forth new growth, and where one shoot had been cut, three or four new ones would grow. The trees themselves remained stunted, and thus, over the years, the deer unwittingly increased the amount of food available to them. Their browsing also let in the light, and their hooves poached the forest floor, so that around the trees grass grew, fertilized by the droppings of the deer.

Brambles and briar roses used the young trees for support, climbing up in search of the light, and these too the deer cropped, biting back the young shoots until their lips felt the prick of the thorns. Ivy clung to the trunks of the older trees, and this plant the deer relished above all others, standing on their hind legs to reach the bitter green leaves.

No ivy leaves grew within six or seven feet of the ground. Below this height the thick hairy stems were bare, for only out of reach of the deer could the dark green leaves give way to lighter green, and the yellow flowers of autumn turn to the dark fruit of the winter. Indeed it was a miracle that the ivy plant could escape the attentions of the deer long enough to climb out of their reach.

Higher in the wood, just within the shelter of the hill, where the wind could not reach, the oaks were spindly and short. Beneath them grew a carpet of whortleberries, small-leafed plants that in the high summer bore a rich harvest. Throughout the year the deer grazed the young shoots, so that the whortleberries never grew more than a foot above the ground, but their branches formed so dense a mat that no other plant could grow.

The deer ate and grew fat, building up their strength for the long winter that lay ahead. Each day it grew progressively colder, and on the shortest day of the year snow began to fall, at first in brief flurries, and then steadily. The deer moved like ghosts through the woods, snow clinging to their hides and rimming their eyes with white.

After the snow came frost, bringing clear nights and a biting wind that drove the sheep and ponies off the moor into the shelter of the woods. More deer came, too, all competing for the now meager supply of food. As the herds scraped at the snow, digging down to find what little food they could, Half Ear read the signs. That evening she led her band away, down out of the woods to the farmlands in the valley.

Here were fields of kale and cabbage, winter food for the cattle, and the deer raided the lush green, at first feeding avidly, and then one by one turning away, their abdomens bloated and tender with the colic that the unaccustomed greenstuff had provoked. More to their liking was a field of turnips that the farmer was growing as feed for his ewes when lambing time came. They ate the tops, and bit the roots down to ground level. The frost held most of the roots fast, but where a turnip came loose the deer were unable to hold it to bite from it. So they left the damaged roots to spoil on the ground, and the farmers shook their heads in anger at the havoc the deer had wrought.

3

The Revelations of Isaac

Deer damage was a common subject of discussion in the Wheatsheaf, the small, thatched, whitewashed inn that stood at the crossroads. One evening Arthur Feather spied one of the huntsmen leaning against the bar, and called to him across the room. "When are you bringing hounds out our way, young Dick? Time you stirred those woods up a bit, isn't it?"

Dick smiled. "Deer giving you trouble then, Arthur?" he asked.

"They're eating all my winter keep, that's all," retorted the farmer. "I shan't have a turnip left when my ewes start to lamb."

"Then we shall have to do something about it." Dick laughed, and swirled the whiskey round in his glass. He knew that the Hunt was due to meet close by Arthur's farm the following week, but he didn't say so. It didn't do any harm to let the farmers think the Hunt was at their beck and call.

Arthur grunted and made his way over to the fire, settling himself on the high-backed oak bench beside the blazing beech logs. He was a short, squat man, as slab-sided and red as one of his own bullocks, with small dark eyes sunk deep in the flesh of his face. He buried his nose in his beer and drank deep.

"Why don't you shoot the deer if they do so much damage?" asked a voice.

Arthur started, almost spilling his beer, then his look of astonishment turned to a slow grin of recognition. "You must be Duncan Turner, that married young Marjorie. You've just come to live at Slade Farm, haven't you?"

"We only moved in the other day," replied Duncan. "I believe we're neighbors. I'm sorry I haven't had a chance to make your acquaintance before, but you can guess what it is like moving farms."

Arthur nodded. "You're from Sussex, I hear. That's quite a distance to come. I expect you find our ways a bit strange to you."

Duncan laughed. "I admit I find some of them a bit puzzling. Especially this question of deer and the damage they do. If the deer are so numerous, why not shoot them, or, better still, why not invite wealthy sportsmen to come and stay on our farms, shoot the odd deer, and pay for the privilege? In that way we could make a profit out of the deer, instead of suffering a loss."

For a moment Arthur sat pondering, slightly shaken by the novelty of the young man's suggestion. Privately he thought the idea a good one, and he felt a faint stirring of greed as he considered the ripe pickings to be made out of rich sportsmen. Then suddenly he was aware that the room had gone quiet. Everyone had heard Duncan's question and they were waiting for a reply.

"I'll tell you what I think," he began slowly, "and you must forgive my plain speaking, but you are a stranger in these parts and don't understand our ways. Hereabouts we hunt deer, we don't shoot them. It's a way of life for us, a chance to meet our neighbors and ride over the moor. The death of one deer, if we catch one, provides a day's sport for a lot of folk. Then there's the venison. We all get a share. Besides, hunting brings money to the area too, what with visitors who come to see the sport, and the horses and saddlery and all that. Your idea is unneighborly don't you see? It would mean the death of a deer for each man's bit of sport, and soon there would be too few deer left to go round."

Pausing for breath, Arthur picked up his empty glass and squinted into it. A speech like that deserved another drink, he thought.

Duncan took the hint and, when he had refilled Arthur's glass, said, "I hear there's a society, what's it called? . . . The League for the Abolition of Blood Sports. They would like to see hunting banned by law. What do you think would happen then?"

35

Arthur stared hard at Duncan, wondering if the young man was trying to make a fool of him in front of the assembled crowd, but Duncan sat, his short, coppery hair aglow in the firelight, his blue eyes intent and sincere, waiting for an answer. Arthur stared round the room, and with relief spotted a familiar face grinning at him over Duncan's shoulder. "Don't ask me," he muttered. "Ask him. This is your other neighbor, Ted Sheratt. Ted, meet Duncan Turner."

Ted Sheratt stretched his long lean frame and scratched his thinning hair. "The League for the Abolition of Blood Sports," he echoed. "We don't take any notice of them round here. If they had their way the deer would be left to breed until they ate their way into starvation. Deer have to be controlled same as any other vermin."

"But supposing hunting was banned," persisted Duncan. "What then?"

"Twouldn't never happen," said Ted emphatically. "Folks would raise too great an outcry. But if it were, every man who owned a shotgun would be out raking the hills, and within a twelvemonth the only deer left would be a few maimed cripples."

"But the deer could be protected surely," protested Duncan, "and controlled by expert marksmen, who could reduce their numbers in a humane manner?"

The drink was making Arthur expansive. He sat back and smiled. "First of all you'd have to find your marksmen, whoever they might be, and then teach them to know the moor, and the ways of the deer, as well as we who have lived here all our lives. Then," he announced importantly, "you'd have to change the law. As it is the deer on my land are my property, and if anyone came after them on my land with a gun I'd have him for armed trespass. If he shot one I'd have him for poaching."

A quiet voice from the bar broke into the conversation. It was Dick, the huntsman, who had been listening in silence all evening. "You spoke just now of marksmen who could control deer in a humane manner. Are you suggesting that hunting is cruel?"

"Are you suggesting it isn't?" snapped Duncan.

"I'm telling you it isn't," smiled Dick, strolling over with his glass in his hand. "No more cruel than herding sheep with a sheepdog, or driving cattle to market. Our way, the deer is killed clean, or lives and gets clear away. Your way, the deer could be wounded, and lost somewhere in the woods, to die miserably, or else live on, crippled, or suffering from maggot-infested wounds."

Duncan spread his hands in mock surrender. "I must say, you all make out a pretty strong case in favor of hunting. . . . And yet, I confess I still wonder." He frowned, staring into the fire, trying to crystalize his thoughts. "I've been a farmer all my life. I was brought up to kill rats around the barn, break the backs of rabbits at harvesttime, and shoot the wood pigeons that came to raid the grain. To me killing is just a necessary job of work, to be carried out as quickly and efficiently as possible. I can see that killing a deer is no different from killing a rabbit, or a rat, or even a mosquito, so why make such a . . . such a ritual of it? Why hunt?"

There was an uneasy silence in the bar. "I'll tell you

why I hunt," began Dick. "It's my job, for one thing. . . ."

"I'll tell you why they hunt, even if no one else will." The voice came from a dark corner of the room, where a man had sat drinking all evening, a silent witness to the debate. A low murmur of disapproval rippled through the bar. "Oh Lord! Who woke the preacher?" "Go home, Isaac, and sleep it off."

Isaac stood up, and his vast bulk seemed to fill the room. Beer flew in a fine misty spray and the glasses shook as he pounded the table with his first. "I'll tell you the truth, young man. Hereabouts they hunt the deer for joy, the same fierce joy that drove primitive man to hunt for food. It's an age-old instinct, the same force that drives a cat to hunt a mouse, or a hawk a sparrow, older even than the urge to till the soil. It's a powerful one too. It had to be to drive primitive man from the comfort of his cave, to overcome fear and idleness and dislike of hardship. You can't uproot an instinct like that in a few thousand years of so-called civilization."

A shout of laughter greeted this outburst. "Come off it, Isaac. Times change you know. We're not all dressed in skins and furs now. Poor old fool."

"Aye! Times change, but man does not, and the pages of history show him for what he is . . . the great destroyer. I am old, bloody old, older nor any of you, yet I was young once, and strong, strong enough to break the bones of a man, to carry weights none of you today could even lift. I've been poor, too. I've never had a motor car, or more than one suit of clothes at a time. But

38

I've been rich, too, rich as the land that bore me. I've seen the farms and gardens bursting with food. There were rabbits for the taking, but they're mostly gone. Once the bays and rivers teemed with fish. You could walk dry shod across the backs of the spawning salmon. Where are they now? Dead, and those that are left are rotting away with a canker no one can cure, and the red sores eat into their flesh. Aye! I've seen change, only I call it destruction."

He drained his glass and slammed it down on the table in front of him. He stood with fist upraised, and everyone present wondered what was coming next. "I'll tell you why we hunt the deer." His voice dropped to a harsh whisper, scarcely audible above the crackle of the fire. "We are still pagans at heart, and we fear the land we have wronged so much. The land cries out for the red blood of the slain, and we offer the deer as a ritual sacrifice. But the blood of the deer is not enough. The time will come when it will demand our blood, and that time is not far short."

He paused, and stood swaying in the heat of the room, his dark eyes burning in the yellow glare of the light. "I know, for I have lived a long time, and I have seen the glory of this land wither and die like the bracken on the hill."

An ironic cheer greeted these last words, and all at once Isaac's shoulders sagged. His head dropped, and suddenly he looked old and tired. "I appear to have outstayed my welcome again," he muttered. "I'll bid you all good night!"

He walked slowly out of the room, and in the silence

that followed Dick turned to Duncan. "I must apologize for Isaac," he murmured. "I hope you don't take his views as characteristic of our community."

"Is he often like this?" queried Duncan.

"I thought he was in extra good form tonight," Dick said with a smile. "He's a tragic case really. He lost his wife in childbirth, and lives alone. When he has drink in him he is apt to go on a bit. That's all really. It's getting late. Can I give you a lift home?"

Duncan thanked Dick but declined his offer of a lift. It was but a short walk to his farm, and he hoped that the exercise and the cold night air would help to blow the beer fumes from his head. He set off at a brisk pace up the lane, his footsteps ringing on the icy road, and soon he was plunged into the shadow of the trees.

Suddenly he stopped, and stood still, listening. Was he mistaken, or could he hear voices ahead? They came again, this time loud and clear. Somewhere angry words were being exchanged. As he hesitated Duncan heard the sounds of a scuffle, and then a cry of mingled pain and anger. The sound was vaguely familiar.

Duncan waited no longer. Breaking into a sprint, he rounded the corner, and there in the road he could just make out the unmistakable bulk of Isaac, struggling with two figures. Duncan seized the nearer, and, swinging him round, hammered him to the ground with short, savage blows from his powerful fists. Then he turned to help Isaac.

At once he saw he need not bother. Isaac had hold of his assailant and was swinging him high above his head.

40

With a grunt and a heave the old man threw his attacker into the ditch. Both men lay where they had fallen, whimpering and moaning with pain, but as Isaac approached with a menacing growl, they scrambled to their feet and staggered off back down the road toward the inn.

"Are you hurt?" asked Duncan.

"I thank you, no," replied Isaac, dusting himself down. "It was nothing. Just a couple of village hoodlums thinking to make sport of mad Isaac. They won't try again."

"All the same," said Duncan, "I'll see you safely on your way."

"I'd appreciate that," replied Isaac, as they set off up the road, "not because I fear further attack, but because I'd enjoy the pleasure of your company, especially since you strike me as the sort of man who prefers to walk alone."

They walked in silence for a while. Duncan was surprised to find that in spite of an evening's heavy drinking, followed by the exertions of the fight, the old man was as vigorous as ever and set a pace Duncan found hard to maintain.

"You don't look like the kind of man who takes advice readily," said Isaac after a while, "but perhaps you'll heed an old man's warning."

"I'll certainly listen."

"Then hear this. Don't trust your neighbors, and don't look to them for help. By that of course I don't mean the sort of hand one farmer gives another, like with the hay, or at lambing time, but support and loyalty in time of need."

In the years to follow Duncan was to wish that he had heeded the warning. Now, puzzled, he merely remarked, "But they are my wife's people. I hope in time to become one of them."

"That you'll never do," said Isaac emphatically, and once again silence fell.

The road fell away and wound downhill, to a hollow where a bridge crossed a stream. Here Isaac stopped and pointed down a rough track. "My way now lies down that path," he announced. "My cottage is about fifty yards away. Would you care to join me in a last drink?"

Reluctantly Duncan declined. "My wife will be wondering where I am as it is," he explained.

Isaac sighed. "My life is free from such problems, but I understand. If at any time I can be of help, please come and see me. Oh, and one other thing."

Isaac paused, seemingly weighing his words, and Duncan waited, listening to the splash of water over the stones, and the soft moan of the north wind as it stirred the trees. "If you have trouble with deer, any trouble, don't go to the Hunt, or ask your neighbors. Say nothing, but come to me. I know who to call."

Duncan was tempted to ask the old man what he meant, but before he could utter a word, Isaac had vanished into the night, and Duncan was alone. He walked on, more slowly now, under stars bright with frost fire. All around him the wooded hills lay crouched like shaggy beasts against the sky, and it seemed to him that the earth was awake and watchful, aware of the countless small beings that moved or crawled across it. The night whispered and breathed with small sounds, as it had done through the centuries, and the earth listened, unfeeling, impersonal.

4

The Lean Days

Above the shores of the Severn sea the wooded cliffs climb high, until they tower a thousand feet above the waves that pound the rocky shores. The woods are dark, sunless, seemingly impenetrable, but here and there the defenses are breached by the foaming streams that over the centuries have cut their way down through the stony red soil, creating steep-sided valleys.

Through these valleys the deer infiltrated the ramparts of the moor, journeying along the sides of the streams, or climbing the steeply wooded sides of the combes to raid the arable land that lay between the valleys and the high moors. In this way they moved from valley to valley, always following the trails of their ancestors, ancient pathways often adapted by man and widened for his own use. They moved with unhurried speed over the rough terrain, making in hours a journey over which a man on foot might toil all day. A valley which was full of deer one day could be utterly deserted the next.

One afternoon early in the new year, Half Ear and her band were sheltering at the head of a valley, shielded from the wind by the massive slab of the moor, as it swept upward to the sky. The cold had given way to a slow thaw, the nights brittle with frost, the days cold and dank, with a chill wind that shook icy moisture from the moss-laden branches of the oaks. Snow lay white and forgotten in the sunless hollows, and the tops of the moors were lost in the clouds.

Some of the deer lay dozing, couched amid the faded fern and the oak leaves that matched so well the russet gold of their winter coats. Rhus and his mother were stripping bark from a young ash tree. Like cattle, the deer were without incisor teeth on their upper jaws, having instead a horny pad of gristle with which to grip their food. They could not bite, but they used the teeth in their lower jaws like chisels, gouging a strip of bark upward, until they could grip it and tear it off. In this way they damaged many young trees, and some, completely ringed round by the attentions of the deer, died as a result.

Suddenly, Half Ear raised her head and stood alert, listening. Far away she could hear the faint clamor of the hounds, and the low thunder of horses' hooves. For

45

a moment she wondered whether to move, but the sounds faded in the distance, and she relaxed again.

The Hunt had met that morning, and in a neck of the woods two miles away had roused a hind. Scent was good on the thawing ground, and the pack had gone away in full cry, but the hind, instead of keeping to the lowland woods, had run straight for the high moors, where the thick mist swirled and eddied over the hills.

Here, amid the deep snowdrifts that still lingered on the bare, windswept slopes, the hounds lost her, and the huntsmen, baffled by the mist, and floundering in the soft wet snow, soon abandoned the hunt, concentrating instead on trying to collect the scattered hounds. By nightfall three hounds remained unaccounted for.

The straying hounds spent a cold night huddled together beneath an old stone bridge. With the dawn they woke, querulous and hungry, snapping and snarling at each other as they emerged into the light of day. They followed the stream down over the moors and so came to the woods. Before long one of them picked up the scent of a deer, and, belling loudly, the three hounds followed it, tails waving and noses pressed to the ground.

So for Half Ear and her band began a long day of harassment. Hinds and calves panicked and ran as the hounds, lacking in leadership and direction, followed first one trail and then another, lost in a maze of scents that hung strong on the damp leaf mold.

Three times Half Ear led the herd away as she heard the cry of the hounds. Their hooves drummed the ground and their hearts hammered as they ran, tongues lolling and eyes rolling with fear, until the hideous noise died away in the distance. The slow-moving hounds had no hope of catching the fleet-footed deer, unless they singled one out and ran it to exhaustion, but the deer did not realize this, and the hounds were too young and inexperienced, too baffled by the bewilderment of scents, to select one individual as their quarry.

On the third occasion, quite by chance, Half Ear led the herd through a thicket where a young stag lay. He was nervous and irritable, upset by the continual clamor that had echoed through the woods all day, yet he was reluctant to leave his shelter. As the hinds thundered by he got to his feet, and stood watching the three hounds as they toiled uphill.

To the stag the hounds offered little threat of danger. They were small, and they were few in number, unlike the large packs, accompanied by horsemen, with which he was more familiar. He stood his ground and waited, as the hounds, still in full cry after the hinds, came nearer.

He attacked before the hounds were even aware of his presence, exploding out of the thorn with a flurry of hooves, his head low and his antlers swinging in a scything arc that caught the leading hound, impaling her on the long brow tines. The impetus of his charge scrubbed the hound along the ground for several yards before her body thudded against a tree stump. Then the points sank home, forcing through hide and muscle and bone and stopping her heart.

The stag shook her off and turned to face the other hounds, but they, utterly demoralized, turned and fled.

They ran until they were out of the wood, and they wandered the fields until they came to a farmhouse, where they were rested and fed, until the Hunt came to collect them.

The stag watched them go, and then turned back to the corpse of the first hound. For a while he played with the body, worrying it and thrashing it around in the undergrowth. At last, tiring of it, he left it for the ravens and wandered away, in search of peace and solitude once more.

The winter dragged on, and the land lay at the mercy of the winds that swept across the bleak and barren hills. Snow fell frequently, in heavy blizzards that buried roads and isolated farmhouses. Sheep died, as, heavy with their unborn lambs, they huddled in the shelter of the high beech hedges, waiting for the storm to pass or bury them in its white drifts. The farmers found some by probing the snow with long poles, or by spotting the small blowholes kept open by the warm breath of the ewes. Others remained lost until the melting snow revealed their last hiding places.

The snows claimed one victim from Half Ear's band. At the head of a valley stood a large farm. The owner was wealthy. His bullocks fattened well, and his sheep prospered, so he could afford to guard his land with a stout fence. All round the perimeter of his farm he had driven long stakes into a four foot mound, and to the stakes he had fastened sheep wire, another four feet of wide-meshed netting. Above that he had strung barbed wire, so forming a formidable barrier, keeping the deer out, and his sheep in. He maintained the fence regularly, renewing any sections that were growing rusty or worn.

He took pride in his farm, believing that neatness led to efficiency, and so he used the oak woods beyond the deer fence as a dumping ground for all his rubbish. The ground beneath the oaks was littered with imperishable junk, sheets of corrugated iron, old cans and drums, bottles, jars, and old bedsteads. The litter lay spread over a wide area, and every now and then a tractor and trailer would bring a fresh load. The latest addition was a loosely coiled roll of old sheep netting, rusty and broken in places, which had been flung down against an oak.

On a moonlight night in February, as the land lay locked in the grip of a hard frost, Half Ear led the herd through the snow, patiently seeking for some small weakness in the fence. Badgers often undermined the defenses, partly by tearing away the soil and stones of the mound, and partly by forcing the sheep netting up with their strong shoulders. If she could find such a gap, however small, Half Ear knew she could enlarge it, forcing and wriggling her way through until the breach was wide enough for her to pass through and for the others to follow.

The snow had buried the piles of rubbish, drifting against it and rising up like the waves of a frozen sea. The roll of sheep netting lay hidden, lost in a high mound of hard-packed snow that had drifted up against the trunk of the tree. Above the ground, and within easy reach of the top of the snow-covered mound, ivy hung in long tendrils, green and tempting.

49

One of the calves jumped nimbly on to the mound and began to tear at the ivy. The snow held her weight, her hooves sinking only slightly as she pulled at the leaves. She reached still higher, resting her hooves against the trunk of the tree and stretching her neck upward, throwing all her weight on to her hind legs.

The hard crust of snow broke, and her hind legs slid down, into the entangling web of the wire. She tried to draw free, and next moment her front feet were inextricably trapped. The broken rusted ends of the wires scored deep into the skin of her legs, and the pain brought a sudden lurch of fear. In a violent paroxysm of strength she tried to jump clear, and then she screamed as the bones of her hind legs snapped.

The rest of the herd looked on, bewildered and helpless, as the young calf struggled and moaned. After a while she lay still, and the herd moved on, leaving only the mother to keep solitary vigil. The moon sank, and the shadows of the oaks lengthened in the snow as the stars blazed whiter in the sky. The cold deepened, and gently the frost eased the calf's pain. She grew drowsy and slept, the warmth of her body seeping out into the snow, until at last the frost laid icy fingers on her heart, so that it beat no more.

As the rose-colored light of dawn stained the snow, the waiting hind moved away into the trees, calling softly to the still figure that lay beneath the oak. There was no answer, and she moved farther away calling again for her calf to follow. At long last the trees swallowed her up, and later that day she rejoined the herd.

She seemed to have forgotten her calf, but, occasionally in the days that followed, she would raise her head and stand listening, in the silence of the snows and the sleeping oaks.

5

The Raiders in the Grain

The long winter passed, and spring came, at first slowly and hesitantly, sheltering in sunny hollows and spreading along the banks and hedgerows. As the days passed, spring climbed out of the combes and up on to the high moors, nurtured by the sunlight and fostered by the warm wind that blew from the south.

April came, and May, and still Rhus stayed on with the herd. Several of the hinds were heavy with calf, and ravenous after the winter, but now there were rich pickings to be found, as everywhere new growth thrust forth.

Half Ear had fallen lame. Some weeks previously a

horse had cast its shoe as its owner was riding it through the woods. The rider led his limping mount home, leaving the shoe lying half hidden in the undergrowth, with several spiked nails pointing upward. Half Ear had trodden on the shoe, and one of the nails had pierced her hoof, passing up between the horny plates and penetrating the soft tissues.

Half Ear shook off the shoe and forgot about the injury, but the nail had left a pocket of infection, so that her hoof continually throbbed and burned, and pus oozed from a suppurating channel every time she tried to put her weight on the injured foot. She still led the herd, however, limping through the woods at dusk and dawn as she journeyed to and from the farmlands.

In a field close by the wood that harbored the deer, Duncan Turner had planted oats. Half Ear soon found a way through the hedge, and night after night the herd visited the field, eagerly cropping the sweet green grain. The days were long and warm, the nights short, and as time went by and the deer remained undisturbed, Half Ear grew bolder, visiting the field a little earlier each evening, lingering awhile longer each morning, until soon the herd was arriving before dusk and not leaving until long after dawn. To some extent Half Ear's injured foot contributed to her carelessness, for she was reluctant to move far, and then only when she had to.

It was not long before Duncan noticed the damage to his crop. At first he did not worry, accepting the situation as part of the price he had to pay for living with deer, but as the days passed, and the destruction grew more widespread, he began to grow anxious. He plugged the gap in the hedge where the deer were breaking through, and hung brightly colored plastic bags on strings across the grain.

That night the deer stayed away, but Half Ear soon realized that the bags were harmless, and forced a fresh entry in the hedge, a few yards from the gap Duncan had stopped. Duncan was in despair. Already a third of his crop had been eaten, or flattened and spoiled where the deer had lain on it, and at this rate he would soon lose the entire field.

Next morning, before dawn, he lay on the hillside, watching the field through a pair of binoculars. In the gray light of morning he saw the long necks of the hinds emerge from the oat field, where they had lain chewing the cud, and watched them move off into the wood. He saw the leader clearly, an old hind who walked with a pronounced limp.

Over breakfast he was silent and thoughtful, wondering what to do. Then he remembered his meeting with Isaac, and the old man's words, "If you have trouble with deer, come and see me. I know who to call."

Isaac's cottage was deserted, but in the neatly tended garden at the rear he found the old man with his bees. Gleefully, Isaac announced that he had just taken a swarm, and Duncan stood in the sunlight, listening to the contented humming of the bees as they settled in their new home. Noticing the rows of hives that stood on the short grass, he asked Isaac if he sold his honey.

Chuckling, Isaac shook his head. "Honey's too precious to sell, lad. Come inside, and I'll show you what I make of it."

The ground floor of Isaac's cottage consisted of one room, to which a solitary small window admitted a dim light. As Duncan's eyes adjusted themselves to the gloom, he became aware of a state of indescribable clutter and confusion. Books, papers, manuscripts, and piles of old clothing littered every chair and overflowed out of open drawers on to the floor. The table was laid with the remains of a meal, and everywhere there were specimens of natural history, dried flowers and ferns, grasses in a tall jar, rocks, twigs, and a whitened skull which Duncan recognized as that of a badger. Deerskins littered the floor, and from the smoke-blackened rafters hung bunches of dried herbs and stoppered jars.

Isaac laughed. "Living on one's own has its advantages. At least I know where everything is." He swept a pile of books from a chair, and Duncan sat down gingerly, while Isaac produced a bottle and two glasses.

The liquid was a clear amber and slightly effervescent, so that it sparkled in the sunlight that filtered through the dusty windowpane. Duncan sipped and found it delicious, dry, and fragrant, and deeply refreshing. "What is it?" he queried.

"Mead," replied Isaac. "Beloved by the ancients, forgotten by this so-called enlightened age. When it is made today it's usually polluted by the juice of apples. But never mind. Now you know what I do with my honey. Tell me, what brings you here, wasting a beautiful morning on an old man like me?"

"I need your help," replied Duncan. In a few words he told Isaac of the damage done to his grain, and how he had watched the herd that very morning. "I counted ten, all told, hinds and grown calves, led by a lame old hind with a torn ear."

"There's only one answer," said Isaac, as he replenished Duncan's glass. "Knock off the leader, just as she enters the field. From what you tell me, you'll be doing her a kindness, if she's very lame. Then with a bit of luck the rest of the herd will panic and scatter. Lacking a leader to teach them bad habits, they'll probably stay away."

"I don't like the idea," demurred Duncan.

"The alternative is a deer fence," Isaac pointed out.

"I could never afford it. That tongue of woodland borders half my farm." Duncan sighed. "You're right. it's the only way, but there again, I've only got a shotgun, and at that range I couldn't guarantee to hit her even, let alone kill her outright."

"That's no problem," said Isaac. Going over to a corner of the room he rummaged in a drawer and produced a card. "Get in touch with this man, and tell him Isaac Penfold says you need his help. Then tell him what you've told me. He'll do the rest."

Duncan looked at the card. "R. T. Adamson, Photographer." "What does a photographer know about deer?" he queried.

Isaac smiled. "That man knows so much about deer he even thinks like one," he replied. "What is more, he is an expert shot with a rifle. One important point . . . he knows the law about deer shooting, and sticks to the letter of it. He won't come on your land without written permission from you, so don't forget that. It's important."

56

That evening the telephone rang in a photographer's studio many miles away. Rupert Adamson picked up the receiver, listened carefully for a while, and then, after making a careful note of the whereabouts of Duncan's farm, promised to be there on the following evening.

Adamson was a tidy, methodical man, meticulous in all his actions. At intervals the following day he checked his equipment, first cleaning and oiling an already spotless rifle. Then he checked the contents of a small haversack, laying each item out on a table and ticking it off against a list. Ammunition, field glasses, hunting knife, green cotton gloves, rubber gloves, green woolen hat, green net face mask, insect repellent, tape measure, magnifying glass, notebook, pen, forceps, an assortment of plastic bags, a flashlight, a groundsheet, and finally a small cleaning kit for the gun. To this load he added a camera, a flask, and a small packet, containing sandwiches.

He left the studio early, and loading his car, set off to drive the sixty-odd miles to Duncan's farm. He had changed into a suit of green tweed, and he wore rubber-soled boots of soft leather, which laced up to his knees. As he drove he mentally cross-checked his list, making sure he had not overlooked any tiny detail.

What he was about to do was perfectly legal. Indeed, he was a scrupulously honest man and would not dream of deviating in the slightest from the law. His firearm was properly registered and certified and was of the regulation bore required by the Deer Act. In other respects, too, he was complying with the Act. He had the farmer's permission to shoot, and the Act permitted the destruction of deer that were damaging farm crops.

Yet although he was committing no crime, he recognized the need for discretion and secrecy on these expeditions. Deer hunting was his absorbing passion and interest in life. Without the confidence and trust of these few farmers who knew his identity, he would seldom get a shot at a red deer. Not one of these farmers would like it to be publicly known that he had allowed a deer to be shot on his land, for fear of antagonizing the Hunt and suffering the ostracism of his neighbors.

They trusted him, and he never betrayed that trust, never mentioned his infrequent excursions, or admitted knowing any of the farmers. Yet he didn't entirely trust them, for at the back of his mind lay the knowledge that it would only need one of them to deny having invited him on to his land, for him to face a charge of armed trespass, or even poaching. So he always made sure he had a written invitation, signed by the farmer, in his possession before he even got his rifle out of the locked trunk of his car.

He drove swiftly along the narrow roads, heading always toward the setting sun. It needed another four hours before dusk, and he had almost reached his destination, but he wanted a good look round before he chose his site, and then he wanted to be in position in plenty of time.

6

The Executioner

Duncan was waiting for him at the farm gate, written permission in hand. Adamson parked his car, hiding it discreetly behind a thick hedge. Then together the two men set off across the fields, all the while moving steadily downhill, over land too steep to plough with safety. These fields were now permanent grassland, for the heavy horses and draft oxen which had once been used to till the land were now gone, and modern tractors were too likely to turn over on the steep and slippery slopes. Now only the flatter fields were cultivated.

The evening was warm, with little breeze. Already the sun had sunk behind the hill, and ahead of them the forest rose like a wall, the leaves of the oaks dark and somber against the lighter green of the fields. Somewhere a blackbird sang, and wood pigeons called softly from the oaks. Adamson moved slowly, his pace little more than a stroll, so that Duncan was forced to adjust his step to that of the other man's. Adamson knew the dangers of arriving on the scene hot and flustered. He knew that the evening would grow considerably colder and that clothes damp with sweat could be uncomfortably chilling. He knew too that gnats and mosquitoes were more readily drawn to overheated bodies and, finally, he knew that labored breathing and a racing pulse could seriously affect his aim. He took no chances.

By his side, Duncan had stopped and was pointing. "There's the field, Mr. Adamson, and in the corner there, by the wood, you can see the rack where they've broken through."

Adamson took out his field glasses and focused. He could see the gap, what Duncan had referred to as the rack, quite clearly. To the untutored eye it seemed unlikely that anything larger than a dog could pass through, but Adamson knew that where a hind could get her head, her body would follow. The hinds did not jump through the rack. Each placed her forehooves on top of the mound and pulled herself through, resting her hind legs on the mound before dropping into the field. This action had worn away the turf, and the red soil showed clearly.

Now Adamson swept the length of the hedge with his binoculars, looking for any other point of entry. Once, long ago, he had been caught lying in ambush at one rack, only to find the deer had entered by another. He had never made that mistake again. Satisfied that there was no other way by which the deer could emerge from the wood he lowered his glasses and, licking his lip, he moved his head slowly from side to side. What little breeze there was blew from the wood. He could feel its cool touch on his moist skin.

With a grunt of satisfaction he turned to Duncan. "This is fine," he announced. "You can leave me to it now. I doubt if anything will happen for an hour or two, but if you hear a shot, give me ten minutes or so, and then come on over with your Land-Rover."

Duncan nodded and handed over the rucksack he had been carrying for Adamson. Then he turned on his heel and set off back up the hill. Adamson watched him go, then looked around for a suitable vantage point. A low hillock a little to his right took his fancy. His right flank was screened by rising fern, while a few scrubby gorse bushes broke his outline. Carefully he went over the ground for sticks and thorns before spreading his groundsheet on the turf.

An hour passed. He had eaten his few sandwiches and drunk sparingly of the coffee in his flask. He lay, almost invisible in his gloves and mask, watching the rack in the hedge through his binoculars. His rifle, a .30/06 Winchester with telescopic sights, lay in front of him, protected from the ground by its canvas case. He estimated the range at just over a hundred yards. At that distance he knew that a soft-nosed bullet weighing 150 grains would be traveling at something like twenty-six-hundred feet per second. As a marksman he knew that to be an accurate shot was not enough. To ensure a humane kill the bullet had to strike the target with sufficient energy to expand at the right time. If it expanded too soon, it might break up before any vital organ was touched. Too late, and the projectile could pass right through the body. In this case the weight of the bullet, and the speed at which it traveled gave it an energy of just over two thousand foot/pounds at that range. Experience had taught him that this was about right for red deer.

The woods grew darker. The blackbird finished singing and flew down into the hedge to roost. He could hear the sleepy chinking of the bird below him. A pigeon flew to roost behind him, passing over him without checking in its flight. That was a good sign. He must be well hidden.

He lowered the glasses for a moment and looked around him. The light was fading fast, and if the deer didn't appear within a few moments he would have to reconcile himself to a long night's vigil, in the hope of a dawn shot. A faint movement caught his eye. A fox was crossing the field in which he lay, bumbling slowly along as, blissfully unaware of his presence, it sniffed for field voles in the tussocky grass.

With a start Adamson jerked his attention back to the field, and then swore softly to himself. While his attention had been momentarily diverted, the hinds had appeared. Three of them were in the field already, and others were coming through the gap. Swiftly he ranged the glasses over the herd. There she was, gaunt and thin necked, the ragged shape of her mutilated ear outlined against the soft green of the oats. He laid the glasses down and picked up the rifle.

He watched her through the 'scope. She was broadside to him, her head raised. A head shot? Neck? Heart? He waited. Half Ear lowered her head and began to graze, biting off the green shoots of grain. Her nearside foreleg was drawn back and he waited for her to take a step forward. Another hind was drawing alongside her, but at the last moment she moved away. Half Ear took a step forward, moving her shoulder blade so that her heart was exposed.

Adamson drew a long steady breath, held it, and, so gently, squeezed the trigger.

The bullet slammed home into Half Ear's chest, flattening as it tore through hide and flesh and bone. Already it was beginning to break up, and fragments of lead buried themselves in her heart and lungs, tearing the walls of the major blood vessels, destroying the living architecture of her flesh. The remainder of the herd, hearing the flat report of the rifle echoing among the hills, stood frozen in fear, looking to Half Ear for guidance.

For a moment she stood still, paralyzed with the shock of the impact, the last bite of grain still clenched between her teeth. She was conscious only of a hot wetness inside her, and she listened as the thunder of her heart grew to a great roaring that brought waves of darkness flooding round her. She coughed gently, took a few stumbling, disorganized paces, and fell forward. Then the herd panicked and ran for the gap, and in a

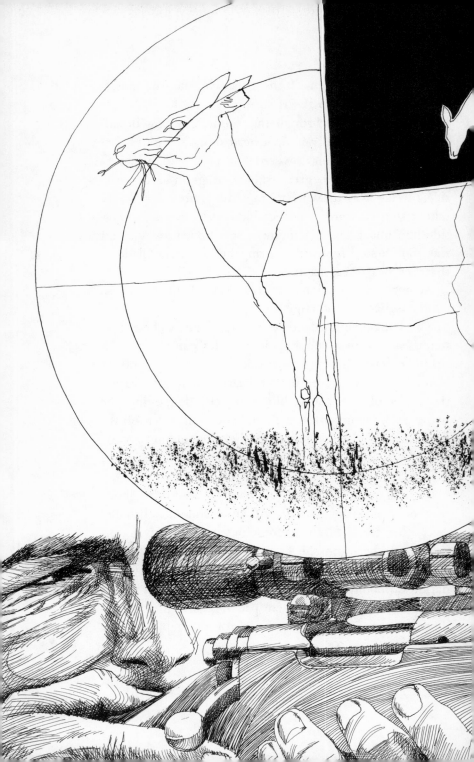

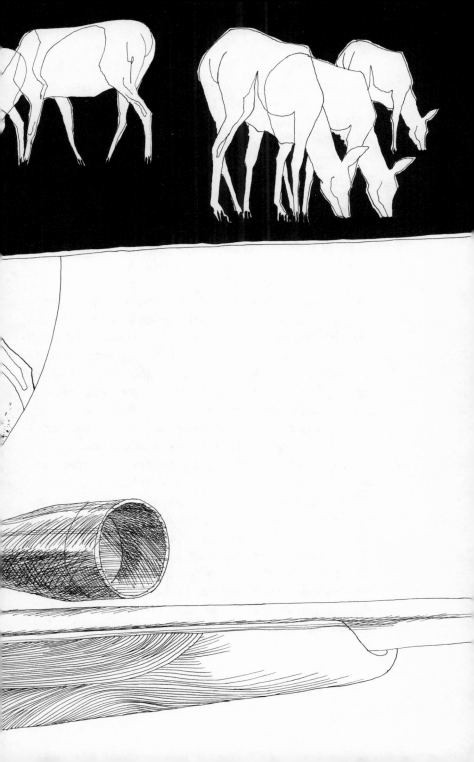

moment the field was empty, save for the dark shape-
less bulk that once was Half Ear.

Alone on the hill Adamson felt relief sweep over him,
the climax of a day of mounting tension. He knew that
if he stood up at this stage he would stagger and fall,
perhaps even be physically sick. Remorse would follow,
and with it the nightmare fear that one day he might not
make a clean kill, that a wounded beast might lurch off
into the night and the impenetrable thickets of the wood,
to await a lingering death. His anguish at this moment
was so real that his body shuddered.

The minutes ticked by, and at long last he collected
himself. In a mood of bleak depression he gathered up
his gear and walked across the fields to where the shot
hind lay. By the time Duncan arrived with the Land-
Rover he was already at work, using what little remained of the light in measuring the body. With the
lights of the truck to aid him he was able to work
more quickly on his routine of self-imposed tasks, looking for abnormalities, searching for parasites, and checking for old wounds. Duncan watched curiously.

"You seem to be finding a great deal to interest you,"
he remarked, watching Adamson skin back a hoof.

"Shooting is a small, but necessary, part of my pre-
occupation with deer," replied Adamson, busy with his
sheath knife. "It would be a pity to lose such a good
opportunity to try and learn a little more about them.
The great tragedy of this age is that we are busy ex-
terminating species without bothering to get to know
them. Look at that. If that were you or I we would be
flat on our backs in a hospital with an injury like that."

66

Duncan looked at the skinned hoof, and the yellow suppurating channel that had eaten into muscle and sinew and bone. He drew a sharp breath of pity. "At least we did her a kindness. I don't suppose she would have recovered from an infection like that. What do you suppose caused it?"

With a few deft strokes, Adamson severed the hoof at the joint, and dropped it into a plastic bag. "Some sharp instrument penetrating the hoof. Probably a nail. I'll keep this, as an example of the damage litter can cause, but . . ." He shrugged. "I'll probably be wasting my time."

"Apart from your own personal interest in deer, do you hope to learn anything of value?" asked Duncan.

"Questions arise," grunted Adamson. By now he had disemboweled the hind, and was searching for internal parasites. "For instance, are deer a natural reservoir for parasites and diseases that could affect cattle?"

"And the answer?"

Adamson straightened his back. "It would be nice to say with certainty that they are not. Truth is, we can't, so we are still looking. So far though, they have a pretty clean record."

"You say 'we.' I gather you're not the only one who is interested in these matters," remarked Duncan.

"There is a small society, of which I am a member, concerned with the conservation of deer, and with promoting interest, not only in red deer, but in fallow and roe deer also. We've managed to do some useful work so far. In fact we helped with the Deer Act, for what it's worth." Adamson removed his rubber gloves, and dropped them in another plastic bag. "There. I'm finished here. What do you want to do with the carcass?"

"If you wouldn't mind giving me a hand with it into the truck," replied Duncan, "I've got a hole already dug for her. I'd like to get the evidence out of the way before my daughter wakes up. Children are inclined to chatter, especially at school."

"Very wise," murmured Adamson, and together the two men heaved the body into the back of the Land-Rover. "You don't fancy a steak of venison then?" he asked, as Duncan started the motor.

"Not me," replied Duncan emphatically. "I'm not overfond of it at the best of times, and she looks a singularly tough old bird. How about you?"

Adamson laughed for the first time that evening. "Believe it or not, I'm a vegetarian."

7

Summer Idyll

Rhus was alone. He stood in the shelter of the oaks and listened to the sounds of the night, the whisper of the wind in the leaves, the thin, dry scratching of a vole, the call of an owl. They made patterns in his mind, but there was nothing in their design to tell him the whereabouts of the rest of the herd.

After the sudden death of Half Ear, the herd had scattered, fleeing in blind panic through the woodlands and making no attempt to keep together. Rhus was strong and swift, and soon he had left the others far behind. The realization that he was alone increased his fear and sent him plunging onward, until at last exhaustion slowed him to a halt.

The sound of water came to him, and he made his way toward it gratefully, splashing into the stream where it flowed darkly across the stones, and wading against the current until he came to a pool where the water was deep enough to lap against his chest. Here he bathed, wallowing and rolling and sending small trout fleeing in all directions to seek the safety of hidden holes beneath the banks.

Feeling somewhat refreshed, he hauled himself out on to the bank of the stream, shaking himself like a huge dog, and rolling again on the short turf. He began to feed, and as he cropped the young growing shoots of an ash sapling, the terrors of the night passed from his mind. He was never to see his mother or the other members of the herd again.

Dawn came, the sun shrouded by smoking pillars of mist that were soon dispersed by the power of the sun's rays. Rhus slept, couched on a bed of fern in a birch thicket above the stream. The morning passed, and the sun climbed higher, until the high moors beyond the woods appeared to lie shrunken and distant against the sky.

The mewing of a buzzard, wheeling in slow circles high above the trees, woke Rhus. The bird had found a thermal and was riding the ascending column of air on widespread motionless wings. As the buzzard circled, its keen eyes surveyed the distant ground, searching for anything, lizard or beetle, corpse of rabbit or sheep, young fledgling bird, for any carrion or small creature which would provide an easy meal. The buzzard saw Rhus, and watched, filled with sudden hope, but then Rhus moved his head, and the great bird sailed on.

The thermal was born of heat, and the heat rose from the wooded combe where Rhus lay. He panted, and stirred uneasily, as the sun beat down with a fierce intensity that pierced the thin-leafed shade of the birch trees and burned on Rhus's flanks. Flies tormented him, crawling in thick black clusters around his nostrils and eyes, buzzing loud in his ears and irritating the thin skin of his face. He shook his head in an effort to be rid of them, and he was aware that his head was strangely swollen and tense. It ached and throbbed, and the bones of his forehead seemed unduly sensitive.

At last, unable to endure the discomfort of his surroundings any longer, Rhus got up, and made his way back to the stream, where he bathed again, luxuriating in the silken cling of the water against his hide. So he passed the greater part of the day, bathing and feeding and slowly making his way upstream. By late afternoon he had left the woods far below him, and the stream was a mere trickle of water splashing over the stones in a narrow rocky defile. The wind sang in the heather and the air was cool.

Evening came, and the sunset stained the faded stones to hues of richest coral. The moors lay dark and brooding, tumbled against the deepening indigo of the sky, and the fissures of the combes were etched in darkest shadow. For a while the world was as it had been after the passing of the Ice Age, before man had come to soak the land in blood.

The stags lay just below the summit of the hill, out of the wind, and commanding so wide a view around them that it was impossible for an enemy to approach without being sighted. Even from above they were safe.

The ground sloped so gradually that from over a mile away a man would be outlined against the sky. The stags had lain at rest all day, enjoying the cool air and the sun, and they watched, with docile and inquiring eyes, as Rhus joined them.

The stags, eleven in all, were in the process of growing their new antlers. Every spring, as the primroses bloomed and the frogs began to croak and spawn in the ponds, the stags shed their old antlers, the older beasts dropping theirs first, the young stags somewhat later. Almost at once, as the bracken fern began to unfurl, the stags started to grow new horns.

The new antlers grew rapidly, arching and branching above the stag's head, until by the end of July their growth was complete. While they were growing, the new horns had a rich blood supply and were covered with velvety skin. Until the blood supply dried up, the antlers were sensitive and easily damaged, so that although the stag could use his growing antlers to scratch his flanks, a chance blow against a branch or rock could injure them permanently. Flies were a constant source of irritation too, so the stags moved out of the wood to the high moors during this time.

Rhus had just begun to sprout his first set of antlers, which was why his head felt so strange to him. During each year of his life he would grow a new set, starting a little earlier in the year each time, and developing a better "head," until he reached his prime. Then, with old age, his antlers would begin to deteriorate. In this first year he would produce little more than the two main beams, upright spikes, which bore the horizontal brow tines.

His mother and Half Ear had between them given Rhus an excellent start in life. Never had he gone hungry, even when snow lay thick on the ground, and so he had every chance of living to grow an exceptional set of antlers. Many factors controlled antler growth—lack of food in infancy, hard winters in later life, and injury, not only to the growing horn. Many a stag had, at some time or another, suffered damage to the bones of one of its legs. When this had happened, the antler growing on the opposite side of the stag's body developed a kink.

Food, the richest and the best, with as much variety as possible, was all important, to give the stags calcium and phosphorus, nitrogen and magnesium, all the salts and minerals and vitamins they needed for horn growth. To fill this need, each stag ate from fifteen to twenty pounds of food a day, according to his size, and the development of his antlers.

Rhus joined the herd and, since they did not molest him, he stayed with them as the days passed and the full bloom of summer spread slowly over the land. All the stags at this time were timid and shy, and more docile and placid in their relations with each other than at any other season of the year. Unlike the hind herds, the stags had no leader, and the group was quite likely to split up, with members moving away in twos and threes, to feed according to the whim of the moment. Yet inevitably dawn found the herd united again, to doze and sunbathe in the remote fastness of their moorland hideout.

Rhus formed an attachment with an older stag, and

the two were constantly seen together, sleeping or feeding side by side.

The tranquillity of the summer did not last long. By
the end of July antler growth had ceased in the older
stags, and one by one they began to clean their horns,
as the blood supply to the antlers dried up and the
velvet died. Tempers frayed with the velvet, as stags
polished their antlers in the tough, wiry heather, or
rubbed them vigorously against a young birch sapling
until they were clean and white. Then, as if consciously
proud of their bright new weapons, they turned in
search of an adversary on whom to try them out.

Rhus, later than the rest in shedding his velvet, came
in for a battering on more than one occasion, but then
he too felt the maddening irritation that led him to
thrash the undergrowth and clean his horns. Then he
gave as good as he received, for in weight and strength
he was superior to many of the other, older stags.

Curiously, he retained his friendship with the older
stag. Rhus had a proper respect for the impressive girth
and magnificent antler development of the elder beast,
while the elder, for his part, perhaps did not regard
Rhus as a worthy opponent. The two stuck together,
and as the herd began to split up the two drifted away
from the moors, journeying through farmland, and hiding by day in any small copse or wood that was large
enough to offer them shelter.

The two stags were at the peak of condition, resplendent in their summer coats of copper red, their antlers
just beginning to darken from constant polishing in the
peaty earth. They moved with an easy grace, tempered
with the hint of dynamic inner power, which threatened

to explode at any moment. Rhus, tall and slender, carried his head high, in contrast to the elder, thick-bodied stag, whose head tended to droop under the massive weight of his antlers.

Months of rich feeding, the choicest to be found in moorland and woodland, together with plunder from growing crops, had made them selective in their diet. In the fields the wheat was ripening, the full ears bronze against the yellow stalks, and the stags raided the fields, wading chest-deep through the stalks, stripping the grain from the ears and leaving the husks. Even when full fed they lingered on in the field, unable to resist the savor of yet another succulent mouthful.

They spoiled more wheat than they ate, trampling it underfoot, and flattening great areas with the bulk of their bodies as they lay in the moonlight, dozing and chewing the cud. This habit of ruminating, of regurgitating undigested balls of food and chewing it thoroughly before reswallowing it, was a habit they shared with cattle and goats.

It served several purposes. If the occasion arose, the deer could graze in an area where danger threatened and waste no time in having to chew their food. They could fill their stomachs and retreat to a place of safety. Yet the process of rumination was of more importance to the deer than a mere safety precaution. Their stomachs were divided into four sections, and in the first two the food was moistened and acted upon by bacteria, which took the cellulose from the food, cellulose which was useless to the deer, but which was nutriment for the bacteria. In turn the bacteria released nourishment for the deer.

After cud chewing, the food passed into the other

sections of the stomach for normal digestion, and so the deer derived far more benefit from their food than they would have done without the aid of the bacteria and protozoa. Furthermore, the bacterial action played a great part in keeping the deer warm in an environment which was often bitterly cold. Indeed, it frequently happened that in the summer the main problem for the deer was to keep cool. This explained their love of water and of bathing, and it is possible that even without the threat of danger from mankind, the deer would choose to be nocturnal, preferring to feed during the cool of the night, rather than in the heat of the day.

Undisturbed, the two stags came again and again to one particular field, Rhus leading the way in the velvet twilight, and the big stag following, his head nodding with every step. Many eyes watched them as they fed. They were seen by hunting stoat and foraging badger, They were observed by a fox, who watched, tongue aloll, in the shadows of the hill. A mousing owl drifted over them, and the nightjar came to flutter round their feet in the darkness, seeking the insects their hooves had disturbed. Once more the stags fed well, unaware that their days of peace were at an end.

8

The Running of the Deer

Another pair of eyes watched the big red stag. In the cold gray light of dawn they saw him leave the wheat field and followed him as he and his companion took shelter in a small wood nearby. They remained on watch, as the seconds ticked by, and the minutes stretched to an hour, waiting to see whether the stag would leave the wood again, or whether he had settled there for the day.

The eyes belonged to a small, unassuming man with a brick brown face and thinning hair, who wore a somber suit of faded gray tweed. He was Platt, the harborer, and his job was to know the ways and whereabouts of the deer, so that when the Hunt met, he could lead them at once to their quarry. He was a quiet man, and in many ways unsociable, for his work kept him abroad until twilight was well advanced, and often he would leave his bed before the dawn. Yet he was likable, and welcome at many a farm, for some farmers considered it a great honor to harbor the deer the Hunt would choose to chase.

Now he rose from the heather, pleased that he had got such positive evidence that a stag was harbored in the wood. So skilled was he in the ways of the deer, so expert in tracking and reading signs, that he could tell from a deer's slot, the imprint of its hoof in the soil, whether it was a stag or a hind, whether it was running or walking, and how long since it had passed that way. Other signs told him the same story, a bitten ear of wheat, a severed shoot from a young ash plant, each small clue told him something of the size and sex of his quarry. All the same, none knew better than he how easily one could be misled, so that he was always happiest when he had had a positive sighting.

Now, to make completely sure, he rode down to the wood, and dismounting, led his sturdy pony while he walked quietly round the hedge that bordered the trees, looking for the slightest sign, in case the stag had left the wood under cover of the trees. Again satisfied, he rode away, down to the farmhouse, where a large breakfast awaited him.

In the dim recesses of the wood the two stags lay, steadily chewing the cud. The dense prickly leaves of a holly thicket sheltered them from the sun, and a screen of tall thick fern hid them from view. Only the tips of the larger stag's antlers showed above the fern. They might have been dead twigs, except when he nodded his head to shake off the flies.

They drowsed in harmony with their surroundings, not knowing they had attracted so much attention, unaware that their short summer of peace was drawing rapidly to a close. The Hunt gave the deer little rest. In the winter they hunted the hinds that slipped like gray shadows through the faded bracken, so cunning and elusive that often they evaded the hounds by their very stealth. In the spring it was the turn of the young stags, three and four years old, very lean and fast, and capable of running great distances without tiring.

Now, in the late summer, as the ripening sun warmed the land, the Hunt demanded the sacrifice of the great stags. To be runnable, to warrant hunting, the stag had to be at least five years old and in possession of all his rights. That meant that his antlers had to have reached a certain stage of growth.

The big stag was warrantable. His antlers curved in a wide arch, reaching up almost a yard above his head. Close to the base grew the two brow tines, long and straight and wickedly pointed. Above them sprouted the bay tines, shorter and slightly curved. Yet a third pair, the trey tines, grew above that, as long and as sharp as the brow tines. At the very tips, the beams divided into three points, spread like outstretched fingers, and about the same size and thickness. He was just over seven years old, and the sire of many calves.

Just over a mile away, a large crowd was gathering.

The site was a parking lot, provided by the National Park so that visitors could park their vehicles and sit in comfort, looking out over the moors and wooded hills to the blue of the Severn sea and the coast of Wales. Every day throughout the summer the park was crowded. Some people left their cars to explore on foot the valleys that lay below. Some just sat and enjoyed a view unsurpassed in the whole of England. Yet others simply read their newspapers, or slept in the stuffy confines of their cars.

On this particular morning, however, the crowd was gathering with a common purpose, for the parking lot had been selected as the meeting point for the Severn Seas Hunt. Since this was the opening meet, the local residents had turned out in force, their vehicles swelling the throng of holidaymakers, who had made their way, by accident or design, to the parking lot and who now waited to watch the show. Small groups of riders waited patiently, some sitting astride their mounts, others holding their horses' heads, chatting quietly, and renewing old friendships. Some were expensively dressed and well mounted. They had come in luxurious cars, their horses following in box trailers. Others, less well clad, had ridden over from their farms. A number of children were present.

Hunt supporters moved among the cars, soliciting funds for the upkeep of the Hunt. The residents gave as usual. Some holidaymakers contributed; others protested vigorously at what they felt was an impertinence. The Hunt supporters passed on, ever courteous, indifferent even to the most hostile of refusals.

Baskerville moved among the riders, welcoming a new face here, or greeting an old friend there. As Master of the Severn Seas Hunt, he prided himself on never forgetting a face or a name. Lean and iron gray, he rode at exactly the same weight he had had forty years before. Since then he had served as a professional soldier, distinguishing himself in two world wars and rising to command his regiment before he retired. Now widowed, his particular pride and joy were his two sons who followed his profession in the comparative luxury of peacetime soldiery.

Now he was free to indulge his love of stag hunting, and on this morning he looked forward to yet another long season chasing the deer over his beloved moor. "I'll never make a penny out of you," his doctor had told him. "You're fit for years yet, and then you'll probably die in the saddle." Which was just the way he wanted things.

With approval he noted the dilapidated bulk of the cattle wagon in the far distance, as it appeared over the brow of the hill. It wanted but a few minutes to eleven, and as usual, he was pleased with punctuality. His huntsmen materialized out of the trees, and with them the familiar figure of the harborer. He rode over to meet them.

"Well, Platt, what have you been able to find for us? A good 'un I hope."

Quietly, the harborer told Baskerville of his morning's work, and Baskerville nodded approvingly, grinning down at Platt. He could not resist pulling the harborer's leg a little. "Not too fat I hope, after eating all that lovely grain. We've got to give all these people a proper gallop."

Platt shook his head. "Don't you worry, Master. You'll follow him clear over the Chains before the day's out, I shouldn't wonder."

Since the Chains were over ten miles distant across the moor as the crow flew, and more than twice that distance the way a stag would run, Baskerville thought not. Indeed he hoped not. The hounds were out of condition, their pads soft and unused to the hard hot heather and rough stones. So, he thought grimly, were a great many of the riders. Too well fed and soft with it. Today would shake them up a bit.

Still, stags just out of velvet and fat with rich feeding seldom ran too fast or too far. His guess was that this one would soon take to water on a day like this and make his way north to the sea.

To the clamor of hounds, the cattle truck pulled on to the parking lot and stopped. Inside, the pack waited impatiently, muzzles pressed against the cracks in the side of the truck, sterns waving as they pranced about on the straw. From the pack the huntsmen called four couples. These were the tufters, old hounds, well trained in the art of hunting, brave, and obedient to command, so that if they roused the wrong deer, they could be called off and set to work again.

The huntsmen moved off toward the wood, followed at a discreet distance by some of the Hunt and a number of foot followers. Other members of the crowd moved away, too, guessing which way the stag would run, and making for high vantage points from which to view at least part of the chase.

The wood lay quiet, a shimmering dark island in an ocean of green grass. Huntsmen and tufters circled round until the faint breeze blew in their faces. Then they moved in, stealthily, the hounds running mute. They would only give tongue when they had found the deer.

Fifteen minutes later huntsmen and hounds met at the other end of the wood. They had been right through without seeing a trace of their quarry. They moved back, and started again, the eight hounds working to and fro, the huntsmen riding slowly after them. For horse and man alike it was hot, tedious work, and sweat streamed off them as they fought their way through the rank growth. Thorns tore cruelly at hip and thigh and shielding forearm. Thin branches whipped spitefully at face and neck, and flies buzzed angrily. In the silence of the woods the heat grew more stifling.

The two stags were uneasy now. They had heard the Hunt and caught the scent. Now they heard the hounds approaching again. The stags lay still, and because they were quiet and cool their scent was poor. Hounds were almost on top of them when the nerve of the younger stag broke. He leaped to his feet and crashed away through the thorn. There was a wild clamor of hound music, the high piping of a horn, and cries of "Forard." Horses thundered by.

Rhus broke out of the wood, almost bowling over two of the crowd. Hounds followed, only to be called in, while the young stag went bounding away and vanished over the hill.

Now in the silence of the wood the old stag moved. He had heard the hounds return and knew that this time they would make straight for the bed from which they had aroused Rhus. He slipped quietly past the hounds. One huntsman passed within a few feet, but did not see him, so still did he stand in the thick cover.

Outside Baskerville waited patiently. He knew exactly what was happening. He had expected the young stag, for the harborer had told him of its presence, and he knew it would be the first to go. An old stag often kept company with a younger beast, rather like a knight with a squire. Some said the old stag drove the young one out to be hunted in his place. Baskerville doubted this, and felt it was more a question of whose nerve broke first. He guessed the old stag was still in the wood, doubling back on his tracks. He sat astride the gray hunter, the first of two horses he would ride that day, and waited. He enjoyed the ritual of tufting—it was like the slow, opening moves of a game of chess.

The old stag had left a trail, faint but true, on the bruised fern and leaf mold of the wood. One tufter found it, quite by chance, and checking, followed it back. For a moment she was unsure, then the musk rose strong in her nostrils, and she gave tongue joyously, running fast now. The other hounds turned and, following, picked up the same trail, each giving tongue as she confirmed the findings of the others.

For a moment the stag stood his ground, facing the foremost tufter and swinging his antlers low to the ground. The undergrowth hampered him and soon the hounds were all around, clamoring and snapping and leaping at his flanks. Suddenly they hurt him and he burst out, breasting the fern and topping the hedge with a single bound. The game was afoot. The Hunt proper could begin.

Once again the tufters were called off, and now all eyes watched Baskerville as, according to the ancient ritual of the chase, he gave the stag law—a short space of time during which the stag could put some distance between himself and his pursuers. Then, at the Master's signal, the doors of the cattle truck were let down, releasing the main body of the pack, and as the bulk of the stag dwindled into the distance of the heather-clad hills, an eager stream of liver and white hounds joined the tufters. Quickly, but without due haste, they were laid on the scent of the running stag. To the clamor of hound music, the riders followed.

The stag did not run far. His first frantic burst of speed carried him easily over the hill, where, once he was clear of the tumult and the crowds, he slowed to a trot, dropping down to the shelter of a small combe. Here he stood, his tongue aloll, his flanks heaving, showing the whites of his eyes as he listened in the silence of the trees. He heard nothing, only the tiny tap of a nuthatch as the little bird mined for grubs in the rotten bark of a birch, and the splash of the stream as it tumbled over the rocks.

His fear abated, and he made his way to the water, lying down and rolling in a shallow pool not deep enough to cover him. Feeling fresher, he emerged, and began to snatch at the lower branches of an ash tree, tearing off the growing tips and bolting them back. Suddenly he stopped and stood, one green leaf still clinging to his lip as he listened.

Far away, rising and falling as the light wind lifted and died, he heard the baying of hounds and the low thunder of hooves. He moved again, without panic, climbing swiftly and purposefully up the sides of the combe, out to where the trees were shriven and stunted by the wind, and the open moors lay baked beneath the sky. Now he ran steadily, his neck stretched and his mouth tight shut, his antlers flat against his back as he settled into the tireless stride that carried him slowly but inexorably away from the slavering hounds, and the Hunt that toiled behind, now strung far out in the shimmering distance. All the time he swung in a great wheeling arc, heading back to the wooded hills of his birth, and the river that flowed north to the sea.

An hour passed, and gradually he began to slow down, as his beating heart strove to supply his mighty muscles with the fuel they demanded. Now he was dropping down, breasting the green fern and thrusting through thickets of gorse and briar, each stumbling step bringing him nearer to the dense cover of the oak woods, and the sanctuary of the stream.

He reached the water, and a dipper flew away with piping cry as he splashed along the shallows. He sank into a deep pool and rested gratefully, feeling the cool water bathe his hide and flow over his head as he let the current carry him down. His hooves touched the stones and he clambered out of the water, shaking himself in a rainbow of spray. He waited, a long time, and his head drooped in slumber, only to jerk upright as he heard again the nightmare noise of the hounds. They were coming down the hill, sterns waving, as they picked their way carefully down the crumbling precipitous slopes.

As he moved off once more it seemed his legs would fold beneath him. The muscles were cramped and knotted, reluctant to obey the demands of his brain. Ahead of him he knew the river fell away, foaming over the lip of a low cliff to thunder into a dark pool below. Silently, sneaking through the arching green branches, he ran downstream.

Hounds checked at the pool where he had bathed, for the stream had broken his scent. Here the Hunt caught up with them as they stood irresolute or searched the banks on either side, and here the brain of man came to the aid of the hounds, leading them on downstream, setting them on the trail again.

He stood in deep water amid the thunder of the fall, and his antlers swung in a wide, scything arc, beyond which no hound dare trespass. He heard the clatter of hooves, and saw the huntsmen as they approached, warily, one on either side. Then the black whips carried by the huntsmen snaked out over his head, the thongs ensnaring his antlers and locking them fast. Powerless he looked for a long last raging breath into the black muzzle of a shotgun, and then the sun went out as his blood ran like smoke into the river to the sea.

Death spared him the further indignities, the ritual stabbing, and the feeding of his entrails to the hounds. His hooves, the prized slots of the red deer, were presented to a pale, rather pretty girl who had stayed close behind the hounds all day. His carcass was taken away, later to be divided among the farmers in the district, and his head, with antlers still attached, was given to the farmer on whose land he had been found.

Baskerville rode home alone, pleasantly weary, his face burning with the sun and wind. As he had anticipated, it had been a short hunt, less than three hours from the time the stag had been roused until he stood at bay. Still, it had been a good chase, with few checks, some good gallops, and enough tricky going to make things interesting. There could be no complaints.

Already the sun was westering, its glare brassy in the afternoon sky. A storm was gathering to the south, and as he passed under the shoulder of the hill he saw, outlined against the angry clouds, the figure of a lone rider looking down on a small group of hinds and calves, sheltering in the fern. The deer stood, necks outstretched, their ears alert, as if querying his business.

The picture stayed etched in his mind as he rode on, man, beast, and earth, the ancient trinity, all interdependent, each doomed without the other. Man and beast were both subservient to the land, and to death, the inevitable. The red blood spilled on the soil and the seed sprouted. It was a bond he felt often, a tie he would not, could not, break. Its chains led back beyond religion, deep into the shadows of the ancient earth magic.

He shook himself. "You're getting fanciful in your old age. Be seeing hobgoblins next, I shouldn't wonder," he told himself. He urged his mount into a trot. He was hungry, and longing for a hot bath.

9

The Exile

After Rhus had bolted from the wood he ran for a long time. His way north, to the moors and the oak woods, was barred by the hubbub of horses and hounds, and people who shouted and waved sticks. So he ran south, following the course of a small stream, which, after a few miles flowed into a larger river.

Here, in the mossy depths of the woods that bordered the river, he found sanctuary, and here he rested and fed. The day, which had started hot and fine, grew sultry, and in the silence of the afternoon the air of the woodlands was stifling under the brassy glare of the sky. Storm clouds gathered to the west, and the distant mutter of thunder set the pheasants crowing in a nearby copse.

Rhus sought the cool of the river, swimming through deep pools lit by amber shafts of light, and wading down shallow runs. Beneath the bank, where alder branches trailed in the sparkling water and the sweet-sour smell of water moss was sharp in his nostrils, Rhus slept.

High on the moor, where the infant river was little more than a peat-stained trickle among the bare rocks, the storm clouds massed in strength. The sky was dark, and a chill wind moaned through the grass, turning the leaves of the sparse beech hedges and bending a solitary rowan with its force. The air was dry, charged with elemental force. Somewhere, eerily, a lone crow called, and instantly the wind died, as if in obedience to the harsh command.

A whiplash of white light split the sky, and immediately an earsplitting bang shook the somber land. For some time the lightning forked among the clouds and the thunder hammered in the ozone-laden air. Then the rain came, a solid deluge that grew and continued as the minutes lengthened to hours.

Rain soaked into the moor, saturating the lichens and the mosses, the moor grass and the deer sedge, the heather, the reeds, and other plants that grew in a thick mat on the blanket of peat. The plants absorbed the moisture, until they could hold no more and the driving rain penetrated the peat.

The great sponge of the moor swelled and went on swelling until it was full. Beneath the peat lay a saucer-like pan of impervious material, and there was only one way in which the water could escape. As the rain continued to fall unabated, millions of tons of water poured off the moor, down the streams which found their birthplace in the upland bogs.

The streams fell away swiftly, and the water swept down with tumultuous force. The streams joined and thundered down to meet the main river, a torrent of water pushing before it a three-foot wave of dirty brown liquid loaded with sticks and branches, tree trunks and stumps, all the assorted debris of summer.

Rhus, sleeping, did not notice the first discoloration of water round his legs. He woke to the roar of the approaching flood. He ran downstream, seeking a way out through the overhanging banks. He came to a wide pool, and plunged in, swimming strongly for a giant boulder that reared out of the black water. For a moment he attempted to climb out on to the rock, but the sides were too steep and slippery. He swam round the slab, seeking a purchase on the wet stone. He was in the lee of the rock when the wave struck, and the current was divided, swirling round to meet him rather than striking him direct. He was picked up and swept away, carried downstream on the rising floodwaters of the river.

For a time he tried to swim for the bank, but always the strength of the current defeated him. Instead, he swam with the flow, his head held high and his hooves cutting the water. Trees and fields flashed by, submerged rocks buffeted his legs, and debris pounded him as Rhus fought against being submerged. The darkness now was almost complete, as the setting sun sank unnoticed amid the gloom of the storm.

Suddenly the river grew calmer, although the current was no less swift. A dull roar echoed above the hiss of the water, a distant rumble that grew louder every second. Almost before he knew it, Rhus was swept over the weir, and was plunging down, deep down, into darkness. He resurfaced fifty yards downstream, in an expanse of water so wide that he could no longer see dry land. Now, however, he could swim, for the current had abated considerably, and he struck out at right angles to the flow. He was growing feeble now and cold with exhaustion, so that when his feet touched solid ground he stumbled and almost fell. The bank rose steeply, and soon he was wading through water that barely rose to his chest, but which seemed to stretch interminably in every direction. Uncomprehending, Rhus plodded on through the darkness, unaware that at this point the river had burst its banks, and that the lake through which he waded had, hours earlier, been a field.

He came at last to a hedge and an open gateway to rising land. Rhus crawled uphill and sank to the ground beneath a small tree, while all around him in the darkness of the night the storm continued to rage. In spite of the discomfort, Rhus slept, and did not awake for several hours.

The rain had stopped, and the sodden earth steamed in the early light of dawn. Bruised and aching in every muscle, Rhus staggered to his feet and, stretching himself carefully, looked about him. The field in which he had slept was filled with rows of small trees, trees laden with shiny round fruit. Tentatively, Rhus sampled the fruit. Here was a new and rare delight. Rhus had never tasted apples before, but he was not one to miss an opportunity like this. Before he was satiated, he had made considerable inroads into the crop, and already he could feel the first queasy pangs of colic.

The orchard in which Rhus sheltered belonged to a boarding school, which lay but a few yards distant, hidden by a belt of trees. Rhus only knew that he was in a strange country, without any way of getting his bearings. As the morning wore on he was uncomfortably aware of the close proximity of man, but since he knew not where to go, and since the pains in his distended abdomen continued to plague him, he remained where he was.

Discovery was inevitable and came in the shape of a gang of small boys, chattering excitedly among themselves as they made their way from the school to the orchard. Rhus leapt to his feet, to be greeted by a chorus of whoops and yells, followed by a fusillade of sticks and apples.

Rhus panicked. His exit to the river was barred by the mob, so instead he took the narrow gate through which the boys had appeared, neatly bowling over the master in charge, who was following the boys at a more leisurely rate. The master kept his head, and lay still; otherwise he would have been felled a second time by the herd of small boys, hot on Rhus's heels.

The way ahead led through a kitchen garden, which Rhus crossed in several bounds. The boys caused rather more damage, and behind Rhus came the crash of breaking glass, as one of his pursuers disappeared into a cold frame. The others came on, cutting a wide swathe through neat rows of winter greens, and pounding root crops still farther into the ground with their booted feet.

Rhus crossed a lawn, and found temporary refuge in a shrubbery of rhododendron and laurel, but within minutes the hue and cry was raised again, the boys now armed with rakes, hoes, and other tools, which they had grabbed from the garden shed. Gravel flew in spurts from the immaculate surface of the drive as Rhus, snorting and wide eyed, fled out of the gate of the school, down a side road, and into the main street of the town, still pursued by a now uncontrollable pack of boys.

Women dropped their shopping baskets, and children screamed, clutching their mothers' skirts as Rhus galloped by. Traffic screeched to a halt, and drivers, imprisoned in the shiny confines of their vehicles, blew their horns and flashed their lights, as, impotent and helpless, they gave vent to their emotions in any form of activity, however illogical. A gang of workmen downed tools, and shop assistants left their counters to join in the chase, while a young policeman fingered his radio transmitter and nervously wondered whether or not to call for assistance.

Now the town lay behind them, and Rhus headed uphill, through a housing development of neat bungalows, with trim gardens, spotless and weed free. Rhus leapt a low wall, and crossed several gardens, rounding the corner of a house and coming rather suddenly on a stout lady hanging out her washing. His pursuers were now far in the rear, and the lady had no knowledge of the stirring chase through the town.

She greeted Rhus with more anger than fear, swiping at him with the garment she held in her hand. The sleeve of the garment caught in Rhus's antlers, and Rhus fled on, tearing the cloth from her grasp. The last his pursuers saw of him was as he disappeared over the hill, the pajama jacket fluttering like a banner from his horns.

The townsfolk gave up the chase and returned to face the recriminations of their peers and the monotony of their former existence. Rhus kept running, driven on by fear, and the maddening flapping of the striped pajama jacket that still clung to his antlers. Several times he tried to shake it off, but it was well and truly fixed, and after a while he learned to live with it. It clung on for many weeks, growing weather stained, tattered, and torn. Three or four times he was sighted, and reported to be wearing it, and small fragments of cotton, adhering to bramble and thorn, marked his southward passage through the fields and woodlands of the lowland country.

The living here was rich, as under the warmth of the maturing sun the fat and fertile land yielded its harvest of grains and fruit. In spite of the continual proximity of man, Rhus lingered on, as autumn gales ripped the leaves from the trees, and winter frosts whitened the water meadows. Down here the winters were nowhere near as severe as on the northern moors, and little snow fell.

Rhus became adept at concealment, feeding mainly by night and hiding during the day. He needed little

cover; a clump of gorse, a thorn thicket, an overgrown copse, even the shelter of a thick hedge was sufficient concealment, as he lay, head stretched out in front of him, and antlers flat against his back, awaiting the coming of the night.

He saw nothing of his own kind, although solitary individuals like himself, and occasional small groups, inhabited Devon as far as the Cornish border. Their numbers were too few, and their ranks too widely scattered, for them to form sizable herds, and they were too often poached or shot at for their numbers to increase. Dartmoor, with its vast expanse of open country, could have accommodated many of his kind, but the greater part of it was too bare and treeless to attract a species that favored a woodland habitat.

Rhus met fallow deer, their hides as heavily dappled as his had been when first he was born, and once a buck, with his curiously flattened palmate antlers, roared a challenge to him, but Rhus ignored the spotted buck, whose bellows were meaningless to him.

From time to time he also met roe deer, their chestnut coats shining, and the wicked, daggerlike antlers of the bucks gleaming in the early morning sun. The diminutive roe, unlike the fallow and sika deer, were natives of Britain, secretive and shy, resisting extermination at the hand of man in spite of relentless persecution. A roe deer could hide in a good-sized garden, and frequently did, wreaking havoc among the vegetables as soon as night fell.

Winter passed and spring came. Rhus shed his old antlers, and as the trees burst into pale green leaf and wild hyacinths spread their azure stain over the floor of the woods, he began to grow his second set of horns. In his second winter he had fared so well that, in size and stature, he would have passed on his native moors for a four-year-old. Yet life in these heavily populated lowland valleys was not without danger. His wandering saved Rhus, and he moved from farm to farm, always journeying on before his presence was detected and plots were laid to bring about his extermination.

10

The Foundling

Arthur Feather kicked off his boots, swiped a cat from his chair with the *Western Morning Times*, and subsided with a grunt. The cat, reading the warning signs, departed for the kitchen, and Mrs. Feather made haste with Arthur's breakfast.

Two eggs and three thick rashers of bacon later, he seemed slightly mollified. Arthur liked his food. Now he sat, picking his teeth and pondering. "Dratted deer have been in the barley again. That's three nights running. They've eaten acres of it, and what they haven't eaten they've rolled on."

Mrs. Feather said nothing. Knowing Arthur, and his

habit of wild exaggeration, she doubted if more than a few square yards had been eaten, and guessed that a lot of the flattened grain would rise again, but she knew better than to suggest this. "You must know where they're breaking through," she ventured. "Why not run some sheep netting across the gap? That'll stop 'em."

Arthur sighed. "They'll only break through somewhere else. I've got a better idea. Tonight I'll block the gap with a charge of gunshot. I'll stop one of them, at least, and maybe persuade the others it's healthier for them elsewhere."

"You be careful!" warned Mrs. Feather.

"I'm doing nothing illegal," retorted Arthur. "A man has a right to protect his crops. Don't worry, I'll use buckshot."

That evening, he went as usual to the Wheatsheaf, and stayed until closing time. Cautiously, he said nothing about his plans, nor did he even mention the damage to his grain. Before he left the inn, he bought a small bottle of brandy, to keep out the cold.

The purchase of the brandy was hardly justified, for it was a warm night. However, armed with his bottle, the shotgun, and a pocketful of cartridges loaded with buckshot, Arthur set off to the field. Dusk had fallen by the time he settled into the hedge, upwind of the gap, and at a point about twenty yards away. Behind him the moon was rising, and a warm wind stirred the trees.

Arthur took a precautionary pull at the brandy, rested the loaded shotgun on his knees, and waited. The young barley glowed softly in the moonlight, and rippled in the wind. An hour passed. Arthur took another long drink and began to wonder if he would not be better off in bed. Thoughts of warm comfort, and Mrs. Feather at his side, began to haunt him, but sternly he put temptation aside. It was still warm in the field, and he was quite comfortable. He settled himself more firmly in the hedge.

An owl drifted over the field. Somewhere a dog bayed at the moon, and small clouds, driven by the wind, drew strange patterns of light and shade over the sleeping world. A questioning, V-shaped head on a long neck peered cautiously through the gap. Quietly, the leading hind pulled herself up and slid into the field. Others followed, dark shadowy forms moving through the billowing grain. Steadily the hinds grazed on the succulent, milky green heads of the barley, neatly stripping them from the stalks. Time passed, and slowly the leading hind drew nearer and nearer to the hedge where, lulled by the night and the brandy fumes, Arthur slept.

She was within three feet of him before she got his scent. For a long moment she stared into the shadows of the hedge, before giving the one warning bark which sent the herd racing for the gap. Arthur woke with a terrible start. For a moment it seemed that the field was filled with plunging deer, and as recollection returned to him, he jumped to his feet. The gun slipped from his knees, and by the time he was fully awake the field was empty.

Cursing, he ran to the gap, and fired both barrels of the gun in the general direction of the fleeing herd. Then, remembering the brandy, he returned to the hedge. The bottle was empty. Morosely, he kicked it aside and stamped off home.

The marauding herd made for the high moor. One young hind ran with a lurching gait, and slowly she dropped behind the others. One of Arthur's shots had scored a hit, and her left hind leg was shattered. The heavy lead slugs had blown away the lower part of her thigh bone, destroying the knee joint, and severing the main artery. Her leg flapped uselessly, and she was losing blood fast.

Now she abandoned any attempt to gain the high moors, and turning aside, she made for the shelter of the oak woods, with their concealing canopy of fern, that bordered Duncan Turner's farm. Faltering now, for she was growing steadily weaker, she picked her way down to the stream, where she drank deeply, in an effort to assuage her burning thirst.

Then there was nothing she could do except rest and wait, as the dawn air grew chill and the setting moon shone small and white in the western sky. Her calf came slowly, for she was before her time, and she lacked the strength to help the birth. For a while afterward she lay still, her sides heaving as her laboring heart strove to give her tissues the life-giving oxygen they craved. At last, obedient to the instinct of her kind, she struggled again to her feet and began to wash her calf. It was too much. Death came and eased her of the burden, and as the sun rose the calf lay beside the body of her mother.

Duncan's daughter Penny found them as she rode through the woods on her pony before breakfast. At first, horrified by the silent, bloodstained corpse of the hind, she was about to ride away. Then she noticed the calf. It lay quite still, gazing up at her with dark, fearless eyes.

Penny dismounted and picked up the calf. As she gathered it in her arms it gave a faint, mewling cry, and then nestled close, without struggling.

The little girl laid her cheek against the calf's neck, and her auburn hair, almost exactly matching that of the calf's, fell in a soft cloud over the little deer. "Poor thing," she murmured. "You're an orphan now. Never mind. I shall look after you."

Tenderly, she laid the small bundle across the pony's withers and rode slowly back to the farm.

"For goodness' sakes!" exclaimed her mother, as Penny arrived at the kitchen door with the calf cradled in her arms. "As if I didn't have enough to do around the place as it is. Take it back where you found it child. At once."

"But it's all alone in the world, and its mother lies dead down in the woods," wailed Penny. "It'll die if I turn it out."

Tearfully, she explained how she came to find it, and Marjorie, her plump, pretty face relenting, bent her own dark head to hide a smile as she stroked the little calf. "We'll have to see what your father says then. Put it in the shed for now, and come and have some breakfast, or you'll be late for school."

Victory thus assured, for she knew her father would grant her any favors she asked, Penny took the calf and made it comfortable on a bed of soft straw, in one of the small outhouses where they kept orphan lambs in the season. Then quickly, she changed and ate her breakfast. By running all the way to the road, she was just in time to catch the school bus.

Duncan laughed when he heard of Penny's find, and went to view the little calf. "It's a hind," he announced when he returned. "Only an hour or two old by the look of it." He shrugged off his jacket and sat down at the breakfast table.

"You're going to let her keep it then?" queried Marjorie.

Duncan reached over and speared a slice of bread with his fork. "Why not? There's little enough we can afford to give her in the way of toys and fancy things. Why not let her find her pleasures in what the country sends?"

Marjorie hesitated, frowning a little as she tried to crystallize what was little more than a vague doubt at the back of her mind. "It's just that I wonder whether we are altogether wise in encouraging her to grow fond of a wild thing like this. Suppose it doesn't thrive? Suppose when it grows older it becomes too much of a nuisance? Suppose it runs away? She'll be heartbroken. Are we wise in making her happy now, only to cause her sadness?"

Duncan pondered for a moment. "If she hadn't found the calf, I'd agree, the best thing would have been for us to have got rid of it. As it is, we're committed."

He stood up, and put his arm around her shoulder. "Pain, and sadness, and grief at parting, are all part of life. We can't protect her from these things. We can't isolate her from life. All we can do is to give her help and guidance when times are bad."

Marjorie nodded and smiled. She saw the wisdom in

what Duncan said. All the same, somewhere in a dark corner of her mind, there was an uneasiness still.

"Meantime," said Duncan, loading his pipe, "I've got to do something about the dead hind in the wood. I've too much to do to waste time digging a hole and burying it, but I can't leave it lying there."

"The butcher calls this morning," said Marjorie. "I could get him to take a message to the kennels. I expect the Hunt could use the carcass to feed the hounds."

"Good idea," agreed Duncan. "Tell them to come just after lunch, and I'll show them where it is."

A Hunt servant came with a Land-Rover, and Duncan rode down with him, over the fields, to the stream by the wood. Already the undertakers of the wild had gone quietly to work, making their own methodical arrangements for the disposal of the corpse. A raven had pecked out the eyes, and in the sightless sockets blowflies had laid their eggs, setting the elongated white capsules out in neat rows, where the hatching larvae would find a ready source of food. Inside the carcass, amid the warmth and darkness and fermenting gas, myriads of bacteria flourished and multiplied.

"Phew!" gasped Duncan as they dragged the hind across the stream. "She wouldn't last long at this rate."

"That's all right, Mr. Turner," said the kennelman. "Hounds'll love this. You want to see what we give them sometimes. This'll be a rare treat for them."

Together they heaved the carcass into the back of the truck. "There was a calf, I hear," said the kennelman.

"That's right," replied Duncan carelessly.

"Bestways let me knock it on the head and take it

along with me," said the kennelman. "It won't do no good."

"Too late for that I fear," laughed Duncan. "My daughter wants to keep it as a pet."

"Is that wise, Mr. Turner?"

"Is it any of your business?" snapped Duncan.

The kennelman looked abashed. "Sorry, Mr. Turner, no offense meant. It's just that you are a stranger to these parts and don't rightly understand our ways. Hereabouts we hunt deer, we don't keep them as pets. I've seen it done a time or two in the past, and always it causes trouble of some sort or other. I was just trying to save you any bother."

"The calf stays where it is," said Duncan curtly. "Now, if you don't mind, I must be getting on with my work."

He strode off across the fields, filled with a sense of oppression and futile anger. He recalled his conversation with Isaac, and remembered the old man's emphatic assurance that he would never be accepted as a native. He hoped the old man was wrong, but ever since he had come with Marjorie to the farm they had inherited from her father, he had been a stranger to his wife's people.

Never for a moment had he regretted marrying the gentle, dark-haired girl, but though he loved the little house nestling at the head of the combe, and though he had a deep affection for the wild, rolling country, with its oak woods, its tumultous streams, and its wildlife, never, he thought, would he feel anything but alien to its people.

What was it about them, he wondered. What single

facet of their makeup set them so much apart from other men? Insular, proud, self-assured, so certain that their way was the only way and that there could be no change, they were as much a part of the land as the oaks that clothed the bare hills, unfeeling, changeless, tough, and unyielding.

Perhaps that was it. They were unyielding. They were courteous, kind, and helpful, with their own code of chivalry, and they would rather die than break it. Go to them, and they would do anything for you, but not one single step would they take in your direction. Never would they bend their path to meet yours.

He sighed resignedly. Perhaps, one day, he might merge with the landscape so successfully as to be accepted as part of it. Sometimes, however, and this was one of them, he was tempted to sell up and get out, to go and live somewhere where he was not eternally regarded as a man apart.

11

Return to the Wild

That evening, Penny jumped from the school bus almost before it had drawn to a halt, and next moment she was flying across the fields, praying that no harm had befallen her new pet. To her joy, the calf was just as she had left it, lying wide eyed and trusting on the bed of straw.

She ran into the house, and flung her arms round Duncan's neck. "Thank you, Daddy," she gasped, a little breathlessly. "Thank you for letting me keep the calf."

Gently, Duncan disengaged himself from an embrace that threatened to dislocate his neck. Holding Penny at arm's length he regarded her gravely. "Now listen,

Miss," he said, "There's one thing you must understand. The calf is a foundling, an orphan, but she belongs to the wild. One day, sooner or later, she will want to return to her own kind, and nothing you can do will stop her. In the meantime, you will have grown very fond of her, and you will be sad when she goes. But when the time comes, you must accept this, for to keep her against her will would be very cruel. Do you understand?"

Penny nodded solemnly, her eyes very wide.

"Now," said Duncan, "we'd better see about giving her some supper. Where's the bottle we use to feed the lambs?"

The calf grew rapidly. At first they called her Spotty, but soon, owing to her habit of being the first to appear when Marjorie called the farm cats for their morning bowl of milk, they changed her name to Kitty, eventually shortening it to Kit. With her dainty ways, rounded head, and pointed muzzle, Kit managed in many ways to live up to her name, but as the days passed, and the calf grew in strength and stature, it seemed to the family that at times they were living with an extremely large and boisterous puppy.

The first thing they discovered was that it was fatal to bend down in Kit's presence. The sight appeared to prompt in the calf an irresistible urge to butt. Penny was the first to suffer, one morning as she was collecting eggs. One minute she was bending down, and the next she was flying forward, face down in the straw, with one hand planted firmly in the basket, which already held a dozen fresh eggs. That evening, the family dined in silence on a large omelet, gritty with pieces of shell, and somehow Penny found herself feeling that it was all her fault.

The school closed for the long summer holidays, and Penny was free to roam the farm and woodlands, in what seemed to be an eternity of long sunny days. Kit followed her everywhere, trotting behind Penny as she rode through the woods on her fat white pony, or splashing through the stream as Penny hunted the small trout in the shallow pools. After one such expedition she followed Penny into the living room of the house, and Penny spent a dismal half hour washing muddy hoofprints off the tiled floor.

More serious was Kit's habit of rearing up on her hind legs to get what she wanted. Her hooves were hard and sharp, capable of inflicting serious damage, and already she could reach up to Duncan's shoulders. She accosted Marjorie as she went to feed the calves, greedily trying to bury her nose in the bucket of calf milk. Rather unwisely, Marjorie tried to save the milk by holding the bucket up high, and next moment Kit reared up, planting her hooves firmly on Marjorie's chest. With a scream, Marjorie fell backward, drenched in warm, sticky milk, into a bed of brambles and thistles.

Duncan, engrossed in the absorbing task of removing thorns from the more tender and inaccessible portions of his wife's anatomy, made the mistake of chuckling over the mishap. As a result, he bore the full force of Marjorie's fury. From then on, Kit was confined to her stall, or the fields, tethered by a long length of fine chain anchored to a stake and clipped to a large dog collar she wore.

She was now fully weaned. Duncan had soon got her

off the bottle, teaching her, as he did the calves, to drink from a bucket. She still had her daily ration of calf milk, and she still stole the cats' milk whenever she had the opportunity, but she didn't really need either. She was omnivorous, sampling the pig and hen food, stealing the cattle concentrates, and sharing the pony's evening feed of oats, chaff, and bran, in addition to browsing and grazing all day. She showed a marked liking for household scraps, and thought nothing of demolishing the remains of a steak and kidney pudding, mixed with cold porridge, crumbs, and stale apple pie. In consequence she was, not surprisingly, as fat as butter, and her sides bulged as she walked.

She still accompanied Penny on long excursions through the woods or up onto the high moors, running like the wind until she had left the staid old pony far behind, disappearing over the rising ground until she was alone in the silence of the cotton grass and the swamps. Yet always she returned at Penny's call, appearing over the horizon with the curious jerky run of her kind, stopping at intervals, neck outstretched, questing the air as if fearful of hidden danger, before advancing another few yards.

At times the young hind disappeared in the woods for hours at a time, climbing precipitous slopes where the pony could not or would not follow, until the trees swallowed her up and she faded from view. At first Penny worried all the time she was missing, but always Kit reappeared, suddenly standing quite close by, statuesque against a background of green.

One evening, as the sunset burnished the gold of the

summer day, and the trees were dark against the sky, Duncan watched his daughter playing in the fields with the hind. The pair made a picture that might have sprung to life from a Grecian frieze, and for the hundredth time Duncan wondered how anyone could bring himself to destroy so graceful a creature as the deer, let alone derive any sort of pleasure or satisfaction from the act.

He recalled vividly the occasion on which this reverence for life had been born in him. The situation was unlikely enough. It was winter, and frost rimed the hedgerows and silvered the grass in the fields. He knelt in a ditch, paunching a hare he had just shot. Normally this was a task to be accomplished with the utmost dispatch, for the smell of the hot entrails and the warm sticky feel of flesh were some of the less pleasant aspects of shooting. Yet for some reason, on this occasion he lingered before tearing the contents of the paunch away from the hare and casting them aside in the ditch.

Instead he looked at the open corpse, and suddenly he was fascinated at the compact way in which the organs were arrayed. He found himself wondering at the complex structure and beauty of the organs, and delighting in the soft hues, the pinks and mauves and reds that harmonized in an intricate color scheme.

All his life he had possessed a strong color sense. At school he had excelled in art, but at that time painting was regarded as a harmless hobby, a bit of nonsense that, at best, kept idle hands from mischief. The stern realities of life upon a farm left little time for such a pastime, and so he dropped it, yet the aesthetic apprecia-

tion inspired by his teacher lingered on. He remembered the slaughterhouse scenes painted by Rembrandt, the sides of beef hanging in the huge abattoirs, and wondered if the Master, in his honest way, was trying to tell the world that here, too, was beauty and mystery to be appreciated, not because he, Rembrandt, said so, but because it was there.

For a long time he lingered over the body of the hare, following the delicate intertracery of artery and vein, admiring the architecture of muscle, sinew, and bone. He shot no more that day, and in the months that followed new fields of perception opened up to him. He was entranced by the exquisite structure of a nettle leaf, a mosquito's wing, the leg of a bee, the jeweled eye of a toad, and out of an awareness of beauty grew a deep reverence for life, for the knowledge that all these art treasures lived and breathed and worked, miracles of miniaturization that no man could copy.

He went shooting no more for pleasure and even curtailed his fishing, imposing upon himself a rigid self-discipline, so that when he had caught enough trout he laid aside his rod, lingering idle by the stream, absorbed in contemplation. There was no self-sacrifice made, no need for self-searching or wrestling with conscience. To kill needlessly was now for him an act of vandalism as unnecessary and wanton as the slashing of a Goya painting, or the breaking of a piece of rare china. He no longer killed, not because he could not, for he still held a contempt for those who, out of squeamishness, were unable to bring themselves to end a life that was suffering, but because he did not want to.

With a start Duncan wakened from his reverie. Dusk was closing in, and already pale stars glittered in the sky. It was long past Penny's bedtime, and he knew he ought to call her in. Yet he desisted, for suddenly it came to him that there was too little time in life when a child could run barefoot and happy through the dew-drenched grass of summer.

One afternoon a few days later Penny set off to gather enough whortleberries to make a pie. She left the pony behind, but Kit accompanied her, skipping and gamboling at her side as Penny crossed the stream and entered the wood, climbing up between the oaks until at last they lay far below. Here on the steep southern slope of the combe the whortleberries grew in a thick green mat among the heather.

The main harvest was over. Much of the fruit had been devoured, and many berries had withered and died, but there was still plenty of fruit hidden among the green. Penny squatted down and began to search, picking the tiny juicy purple globes and popping them into a plastic bag. Kit, after a few abortive attempts to steal the fruit, soon wearied of such an inactive pastime and wandered off uphill.

Absorbed in her task, Penny ignored the hind and paid no heed to her absence. The hours passed, the rays of the sun lengthened, and the bag grew steadily fuller. Only when the shadow of the hill fell across the combe did Penny look up, and then gaze about her at the life-less, empty wilderness of windblown heather.

A mile away, Kit stood with her back to the setting sun, staring intently at a group of hinds. At first she failed completely to recognize her own kind, but the scent of them was strong in her nostrils, and it was deeply attractive to her. She took a few steps nearer and paused, neck outstretched, as the instinct to join them grew in her mind.

At that moment Penny appeared, a tiny figure on the distant horizon, and faint on the breeze Kit heard her name called, once, then twice, and then again. She half turned, irresolute, as the magnet of her affection drew her back to the little girl. She looked back at the hinds, and they, as if impatient, turned their backs and began to move away. As they did so each hind displayed the white of her rump, broken by the vertical black band of the tail.

It was a signal, the command that Kit could not disobey. The banner of her kind was calling her, and at that moment it was as if a steel shutter had fallen in her mind, cutting out all memories of life on the farm, and instantly her love for Penny was forgotten as she ran to join the herd.

Penny cried herself to sleep that night, and next day, and all the next, she searched in vain, riding the moors until her pony was worn out. Even a trip to Exeter, to buy a new dress, with all the excitement of lunch in a restaurant and an afternoon at the movies, did little to comfort her in her grief. But as the days went by and Kit failed to return, Penny gave up searching.

12

Death of a Hind

The hind had been running for over an hour, her hooves sending spurts of water flying from the soggy sour land as she swung in a great wide circle over the moor. Behind her toiled the hounds, clamorous and slavering, strung out across the heather in a liver and white stream.

Baskerville, hunched over his saddle, watched from his vantage point on the hill. He was glad, in a way, that this was the last of the hind hunting for the season. It was a humdrum business at the best of times, a matter of sitting astride an idle horse and waiting while the hounds did their work. Invariably the hind went in circles, or ran to and fro over the same ground, until she was killed but a few yards from where she was roused. Baskerville looked at his watch, and thought about the spring stag hunting. At least he could be sure of a good gallop then.

The day, which had dawned so smiling and full of promise, was rapidly deteriorating. The spring sun had vanished behind the clouds. Up on the hill the air was chill and raw, and Baskerville noticed uneasily that mist was rolling in off the sea. Hind hunting might be necessary, but it could be deuced uncomfortable, and most unprofitable. There would be little return for this day's work, with few riders, and even fewer followers. Still, there had been more than the usual number of complaints about damage to root crops, and a kill would do a lot to lessen them.

The hind was coming toward him, and her speed seemed to be lessening. Any moment now she would be dropping down into the valley, where the hounds should have little difficulty in cornering her. Then a short sharp gallop should see the end of the matter. He collected his horse, waking the bay gelding from an uneasy doze, and began to move slowly down the hill.

Suddenly he stopped, and cursed out loud. The hind had turned aside and was running across the hill, heading out toward the moor again. Standing in the stirrups, Baskerville saw the cause. A fox, which must have been sleeping in the furze, had awakened directly beneath the hind's feet. Now he ran like a red streak, down over the hill and through a field, sending a flock of sheep bunching together in stupid fright.

Baskerville kicked his horse into a gallop. As he rode

in pursuit he saw out of the corner of his eye the rest of the field hastening to join him. Now there was only one way the hind could run, along the narrow strip of moor that divided Duncan Turner's land from Arthur Feather's. Baskerville reckoned the hind would make for the oak wood and the stream that bordered Turner's land.

The going was rough. Thickets of gorse grew amid the tough, wiry heather, and loose stones and shale made the side of the hill treacherous for horse and rider alike. Baskerville gave his horse its head, heard the heavy pounding of hooves beneath him, and trusted his mount to carry him safely over the moor. Already, with a speed that was eerie and unnerving, the mist was sweeping over the land. One moment the way ahead would be clear, and the next it would be blotted out, as a gray veil fell across the moor. All the time the field was gaining on the hounds. He could hear their hungry clamor in the distance. A bare half dozen riders kept abreast of Baskerville, with Dick, the huntsman, riding on the far right.

No one saw the bog until it was too late. The mist hid the treacherous green of the mire, with its deep, dark pools where, centuries before, men had dug peat for their fires. The hind, and the pursuing hounds, had crossed in safety, but the quaking ground could not support the massive weight of the horses.

Only Dick escaped, skirting the edge of the swamp and swinging right onto firmer ground. Through a rent in the curtain of fog he saw that half the field was down, Baskerville choking in three feet of reeking black mire, his horse rolling dangerously near. Other riders were staggering to their feet, their clothes plastered in mud, struggling to lead their mounts to safety.

Dick dared not stop. Uppermost in his mind was the thought that the hind was almost spent and in a matter of minutes the hounds would be all about her. What would happen then, with no huntsmen to control them, he didn't need to guess. He rode on, without any thought for his own safety, risking his neck in a last desperate attempt to catch up with the hounds. His horse thundered over the ground, slipping and sliding as the way began to lead downhill, once stumbling so that Dick fell forward on to his mount's neck. Horse and rider recovered themselves somehow, and now they were in the woods, the horse slithering down on its haunches as Dick raised one arm in a vain attempt to save his face from the branches that lashed like whips.

Down in the valley, Penny wandered by the stream, seeking wild snowdrops that hid among the fern. In the normal way she would have been at school, but an attack of measles had kept her at home, and although she was now almost recovered, she was having a few days' convalescence. A sudden crashing in the woods above her head startled her, making her look up, and then her heart gave a great leap of joy. "Kit," she called. "Kit, you've come back to me at last. Where have you been all this time?"

She took a step forward to the hind as it stood poised on the bank of the stream, and then her happiness was drowned in a wave of fear as she heard the hounds. Next moment she stood in soundless horror as the pack poured round the hind, snapping and snarling, dragging the deer down until she sank to her knees. Hounds bit and tore, shaking and worrying at the faded brown hide, and then came the ultimate obscenity. As Penny watched, one hound took hold of the hind just below her eye, and, almost in slow motion it seemed, tore a wide strip of skin from the hind's face. For a moment the bare bone gleamed white, and then myriad florets of red blossomed and grew until the blood ran down her face.

Penny screamed then, and her cry was heard by Dick as, cursing, he forced his flagging mount over the last few yards. Leaping to the ground he flung himself at the hounds, laying into them with such asperity that they fell away, slinking in a wide circle round their prey.

The hind half lay, half knelt in the bracken, her eyes closing and her body trembling from the shock and pain of the assault. Dick had no gun with him, but without hesitation he drew the long hunting knife that hung at his belt. Grasping the hind's muzzle with his left hand, he forced her head back, exposing her throat. Where the windpipe entered the chest he pressed the point of the knife home, working the haft to and fro so that the sharp cutting edge of the steel carved through the major veins and arteries that lay inside the chest.

With a gurgling sigh the hind died and slid off the knife to lie at his feet. Only then did Dick remember the girl and turned toward her. Penny took one look at the huntsman, his hand and forearm covered with blood, the dripping knife still clutched in his grasp, and she fled, stumbling over the fields, her body shaking with huge retching sobs. For a moment Dick was tempted to ride after her, but then he remembered that he alone stood between the hounds and their quarry. There was nothing he could do but wait, until the rest of the Hunt arrived on the scene.

Baskerville was the first to appear, soaking wet and plastered from head to foot with slimy black peat. As soon as Dick told him what had happened, he mounted his horse again and set off for Duncan Turner's farm. Duncan himself answered the door and stood regarding Baskerville in stony silence.

Baskerville hesitated a moment, wondering what to say. "I've come to apologize on behalf of the Hunt, for what happened down there in the woods." He waved his hat in the direction of the moors.

Duncan continued to stare at him, not speaking.

"If there's anything I can do? We are all deeply sorry that your little girl should have been so upset."

Duncan began to shut the door in Baskerville's face. Then he paused. "You can call the doctor," he said curtly. "That is, if you want to save the child's mind."

Then he did slam the door, and Baskerville rode away, deeply troubled, and desperately trying to make his tired mind think of the whereabouts of the nearest telephone. Eventually he had to ride three miles across the moor, in order to summon the doctor. Then he returned to the scene of the kill, and only when his duties were completed did he allow himself to go home, shaking with cold and fatigue and sick with worry over the events of the day.

It was over an hour before the doctor arrived at the

Turners' farm, and throughout that time Marjorie strove to calm the hysterical child. In vain she tried to convince Penny that it was not Kit that had been killed, but a much older hind, and that Kit was still too young to be hunted in that way.

It was all to no avail. Penny seemed not to hear her, or even to recognize her any longer, staring wide eyed at a point beyond her shoulder, as though she was reliving the scene that had caused her so much anguish. Ever since the moment she had burst into the farmhouse, screaming that the Hunt had killed Kit down by the stream, Marjorie had been unable to get a word out of her, only a continuous dry sobbing during which no tears came.

Then at long last Penny was still, drugged and unconscious under the influence of a strong sedative. Marjorie sat on by her side, even though the doctor had assured her that Penny would sleep through the night and that he would call again the next morning. The shock had caused a severe setback in her recovery from her illness. Her temperature had risen, her skin was hot and dry, and from time to time she stirred in her sleep. Marjorie could do little but hold Penny's hand, and bathe her forehead in an attempt to cool the fires that burned there.

Alone downstairs, Duncan sat brooding by the gray embers of the dying fire. When first he had come to the farm with Marjorie, he had known little about hunting. He remembered how his neighbor Ted Sheratt, an old friend of his father-in-law's and almost an uncle to Marjorie, had pointed out to him that the Hunt sometimes crossed his land. Ted had hinted that Marjorie's father had always approved of the arrangement, intimating that Duncan should carry on the custom. Duncan in the first flush of happiness at being in possession of his own farm, had agreed without giving the matter much thought. If anything, he was anxious to be accepted as a member of this tightly closed community, and eager to make any gesture that would prove him to be a good neighbor. He never knew that Baskerville had sent Ted on this diplomatic mission.

Often since, Duncan had regretted his original decision and wondered whether on moral grounds he ought to insist that the Hunt stay off his land. Yet always he delayed taking any positive action, partly for Marjorie's sake and partly because, after all this time, it would be regarded as a studied insult to the Hunt and a direct affront to his neighbors. As things were, the Hunt seldom came near, and until now Penny had been too young to take much notice. All she'd ever heard of the Hunt was the distant cry of the hounds.

Now the seeds of his neglect had sprung up and threatened to destroy his happiness. Duncan, unable to sleep, decided that he would take steps to make sure that from now on his daughter could enjoy the freedom of her home without running the risk of being terrified out of her mind. He went to the toolshed and got to work. At first light he was erecting the crudely fashioned notices he had made, announcing to the world that Slade's Farm was private land, and that no hunting was allowed.

13

Duncan Bans the Hunt

Baskerville heard the news the following evening, as he rounded a corner of the lane and met Feather's van blocking the way. As his horse drew alongside, Feather stuck his head out of the window of the van. "Here's a fine carry-on then, Master," he announced.

Baskerville grinned down at the farmer's round red face. "What now then, Arthur? Have you won a fortune, or has Mrs. Feather had twins?"

Feather beamed, not at the Master's joking, but with delight at being the first to bring bad news. "You've not heard then? Duncan Turner's put padlocks on all his gates, and notices saying there's to be no more hunting on his land. What are you going to do now, Master, now that hounds can't run through Sandygate bottom?"

Baskerville was doubly annoyed, angry that Duncan should insult the Hunt so deliberately and irritated that he should hear the news from the grinning Feather. As usual, he supposed, he was the last person in the countryside to know. He tapped his boot with his crop. "It's no business of yours or mine, Arthur, what a man does with his own land. If Duncan doesn't want us, we'll go somewhere else. Exmoor's a big place. Duncan's been upset lately. It's a very sad business, and I wish it had never happened, but what's done is done, and I can only hope that time will make amends. Good day to 'ee!" He touched his cap and rode on, leaving Feather to let in his clutch and drive slowly away.

As soon as the noise of Feather's exhaust had faded, Baskerville urged his hunter into a trot and, leaving the lane, cut northeast across the moor. He was worried. This was exactly the sort of situation that had to be checked at once, if it was not to get out of hand. There were far too many Bolshies nowadays, demonstrators and busybodies only too anxious to undermine established customs.

The sun was sinking behind the Atlantic, bathing the high moor in a golden spread of light. Baskerville dropped into the purple shadow of the valley, and, as he expected, found Ted Sheratt looking over his sheep. Tethering his mount to a gatepost he strolled over. "Evening, Ted!" he called. "Looks as though you are going to be busy in a day or so."

Ted nodded. "It should be a good lambing season, if

the weather stays dry. Still, for what profit there is in sheep nowadays, I sometimes wonder why I bother."

Baskerville chuckled. He had never yet heard a farmer admit to doing well. He hoped he never would. "It's in your blood, boy. You know as well as I do you'd be lost without your sheep."

Embarrassed, Ted grinned, and scratched his head without removing his cap. For a moment he squinted into the setting sun, deliberately avoiding the Master's eye. "You're a long way off your route. Did you want to see me about something special?"

"No, no," said Baskerville hastily. "I was just out for a hack and thought I'd look to see if there was a runnable stag up on the top."

"Why, what's the matter?" asked Ted slyly. "Don't you trust your harborer any more?"

Baskerville acknowledged defeat. "Truth is, Ted, I'm worried, worried and upset over this Turner business, and I came to ask your help."

Ted shrugged. "I can't help 'ee," he said roughly. "Mazed fool is putting up padlocks and bars and talking about a deer fence. He'll do it, too, I shouldn't wonder."

Instantly Baskerville regretted rushing into such a delicate matter. "It's not that part that worries me, Ted. I'm sorry for Turner. He's a likable chap and a good farmer. He has every right to feel angry and bitter at what happened, and I respect him for it. It's not what he's doing, it's . . . well, it's the way that he's doing it. All this . . . advertising. Telling the world he's against us."

It was getting dark, and Ted was anxious to be off to

his meal, and the light and warmth of the farmhouse, but he stayed on, stonily watching Baskerville's face in the gloom. He now knew what Baskerville wanted, but waited to be asked.

"If Duncan had come and seen me, put his point of view, we'd have respected it. We would have stayed off his land. As things are now, it's a waste of time my going near him."

He laid his hand on the other man's shoulder, and, as a signal that he had nearly finished, began to lead him in the direction of the farm. "Look, Ted, you're his friend, jolly him along a bit. Buy him a few drinks and tell him how sorry I am, how sorry we all are, that this ever happened. And tell him not to waste good money on padlocks and paint and fences and such rubbish. We'll respect his wishes. You have my word for it."

Ted Sheratt stood and watched the Master of the Severn Seas Hunt ride away into the night. "I'll do it," he said softly, "and you know I'll do it, and I'll be wasting my time, and you know that too." It was part of the ritual, and life in the country was made up of ritual, from birth to death, and from seedtime to harvest.

After he had taken his meal he washed and shaved, and then drove round to Turner's farm. Marjorie answered the door. "It's Ted," she called over her shoulder. "Wants to know if you would like to go for a drink."

Duncan came to the door. He looked tired, and his eyes betrayed the smile with which he greeted Tom. "Come in. Welcome to the leper colony. You're the first visitor in two days. Aren't you afraid you'll catch it?"

"Don't, Duncan," pleaded Marjorie. "Ted doesn't want to listen to our worries. Why don't you do as he asks and go down to the Wheatsheaf for an hour or two. It will do you good."

"Thank you, Ted, but no," said Duncan, sitting down by the fire. "My own cider's good enough for me, and you're welcome to a jar if you fancy it. Arthur Feather was round yesterday morning as I was putting up the last of my signs, and he drove away so fast he must have blown a gasket. I reckon the whole countryside knows by now, and I've no wish to embarrass the regulars in the Wheatsheaf with my presence."

Ted sighed and sat down at the table. Marjorie came in with brimming mugs of cider, and he drank deeply, thinking he might as well get his duty over and done with. What was it that fool Baskerville had said. . . ? "Jolly him along!"

"You've got it all wrong, Duncan," he said slowly. "You'd be just as welcome in the Wheatsheaf tonight as any other night. People do understand, and everyone is very sympathetic toward you."

"I don't want sympathy," snapped Duncan. "I want to be left in peace, to farm my land and bring up my family without my little girl being driven nearly out of her mind with horror."

"In which case it's simple. Just take down all those signs, unlock your gates, and carry on as though nothing had happened. The Hunt won't bother you. They'll stay away."

For a moment there was silence in the room, a silence

broken only by the crash of a falling beech log in the fire. A pungent whiff of woodsmoke filled the air.

It was Marjorie who spoke. "Baskerville sent you." It was a statement rather than a question.

Ted sat still. He felt only relief that it was over. Now he could leave.

"Before you go, hear this," said Duncan softly. "I'm not just against the Hunt crossing my land. I'm against every foul unjustifiable thing it stands for. If my daughter had been violated, sexually assaulted, everyone in the land would be looking for her attacker, screaming for justice. Yet out there the other afternoon in the winter sunshine, my little girl playing in the woods was subjected to such a spectacle of blood and savagery and pagan cruelty that it came close to destroying her mind."

He stood up, and for a moment Ted felt certain he was about to be attacked. Instead Duncan deliberately turned his back. "And we have your sympathy. Go back to Baskerville and tell him it's not enough."

Ted did no such thing. From now on affairs could only get worse, and he still had too much liking for the Turners to wish them further harm. He stayed away from Baskerville, and, as he expected, Baskerville never came near. Even when they met in the market, the question was never raised.

At the end of the week, the notices were still displayed at Slade Farm. Holland couldn't resist having a sly poke at Baskerville when they met in the bank. "I hear there's a middle herd of deer harboring at Slade Farm these days."

132

"Hello, Floury," Baskerville greeted him with a smile. Floury Holland was the owner of Holland's Flour, Feed, and Fertilizer Mills, a firm which supplied half the farmers in the neighborhood with cattle food. Floury and Baskerville had been to school together, so they were old friends. "Let's hope they don't eat Turner out of house and home. Deer aren't paying guests."

Floury sucked anxiously at his walrus moustache. "Indeed you're right there. Deer can do a terrible amount of damage if they are not controlled."

Baskerville sighed. "I just wish none of this unpleasant business had ever happened. Still, it's none of our business now, nor our worry. Leastways," he hinted, "it's not my worry, nor yours as long as he can pay his cake bill."

Floury wasted no time. Back in his office he rang his accounts clerk. "Bring in the account of Duncan Turner, of Slade Farm, will you, George? I'd like to have a look at it."

As he waited, he tapped his teeth with a pencil. How lucky meeting Baskerville like that. Yet really, it wasn't luck. It was all part of the pattern of successful business, knowing people, knowing trends, knowing when to act. A good miller, he thought, chuckling over his own wit, should always know which way the chaff was blowing in the wind.

There was a tap at the door, "Come in," he called irritably. "You've been long enough. Let's not waste any more time."

Ten minutes later George emerged from the office. "That old horror," he complained to Jean, the cashier, "has just given me a roasting because Duncan Turner owes us two hundred pounds. He says I should never have let it get so high, and he is to have no further goods on credit."

Puzzled, Jean glanced at the account. "If everyone was stopped who owed us that much, we'd be out of business. Turner, he's the man who's banned the Hunt from his land, isn't he?"

George shrugged disinterestedly. He was city born and bred. "I know nothing about your barbaric country habits," he answered.

Jean did. She was a follower of the Hunt herself. She mentioned the affair of the Turner account to her cousin, who told her boyfriend, who told his sister, who in turn told her friend as they traveled to work on the bus. That night Arthur Feather spoke his mind in the bar of the Wheatsheaf.

"When I expressed my regrets to the Master, Colonel Baskerville spoke up like a gentleman. Said how sorry he was and how he hoped it would soon blow over. Yet here's this fellow Turner still neglecting his farm and his stock, spreading barbed wire all over the place, and now my own daughter comes home and tells me can't even pay his feed bill."

"Get on with you, Arthur," said one of his audience. "Expressed your regrets! I like that. You haven't enjoyed anything so much since the fishermen threw those beatniks in the harbor. Anyway, how does your daughter know he can't pay his bills? Is she going out with old Floury now then?"

"You watch your tongue," warned Arthur. "If I

was younger I'd have you outside for that." He glared about him at the assembled company. Excitement and the drink he had taken during the evening made him careless with his tongue, and ready to cause any mischief he could. Through the smoke haze of the bar he saw the lean ferret face of Thomas Redd, one of the biggest wholesale butchers in the district.

Arthur took a long pull at his beer. "You mark my words," he said loudly, aware that Redd was listening, "Duncan Turner will be sending his bullocks to market any day now, even though anyone who was half a judge of cattle could see they weren't ready." He sniggered, and drained his glass. "Don't know what sort of a butcher would buy them. My wife wouldn't shop with him, that's for certain."

14

The Hunting
of Duncan Turner

Duncan read the letter from Holland's Flour, Feed, and
Fertilizer Mills with mixed feelings of anger and dismay.
Life had slowly begun to return to normal. Penny was
well again, for the brain fever which had threatened to
develop as a result of the shock had not materialized, and
she had made a rapid recovery. Nothing had been said
or done about Duncan's action in banning the Hunt
from his land, and he had hoped that the affair was
dying a natural death. Now this bombshell had landed in
his lap. Without comment, he flipped the letter across
the breakfast table to Marjorie.

Marjorie frowned as she read the briefly worded message. "What are you going to do?" she queried.

Duncan shrugged. "No use going to the bank for a loan. We're overdrawn already. This couldn't have happened at a worse time of year." He got up and stared out of the window. "I'll just have to send those two bullocks to market I suppose. They're not ready yet, and I expect I shall lose about twenty pounds on the deal, but if I can't buy feed for them, I can't fatten them anymore."

Marjorie read the letter again, and a sudden doubt crossed her mind. Was this part of a general attempt of Holland's to tighten up on their accounts, or were they being singled out as victims? She looked up suddenly. "Don't send the bullocks to market locally," she said. "Send them to Newton Abbot."

"But that's ridiculous," scoffed Duncan. "Newton is over sixty miles away. I've got to make some profit."

Reluctantly, Marjorie let the matter drop, telling herself that her fears were probably all imagination anyway. It was easy to get deluded into thinking the world was against one. All the same, the nagging doubt persisted and worried her as she went about her household tasks.

For the bullocks the ordeal began early. From the clear cold air of the hills they were brought down to the yard, to await the coming of the cattle wagon, and the jolting discomfort of the short drive to market. From all the neighboring countryside cattle were arriving at the market, as the drivers swung their heavy trucks into the yard, to reverse them and park them neatly against the cattle stalls. Then the massive rear doors were lowered, to form a ramp, down which the bullocks lurched, drunken with the ride, and suddenly fearful as they blinked in the bright light of their unfamiliar surroundings.

The drivers, as expert and skillful in handling the livestock as they were in driving their vehicles, coaxed the beasts out, handing them over to the part-time drovers who were employed by the market. Unlike the truck drivers, who were adept at anticipating the bullocks' intentions, and who knew exactly when to time a necessary shout or prod to encourage a beast in the right direction, the drovers were simpler in their tactics.

For the bullocks, the lesson was easy, and one that was quickly learned. Move rapidly, and in the right direction, through the maze of pens, and the reward was peace. Take the wrong turning or balk and refuse to move and the punishment was a rain of blows directed at the most accessible part of the beast's body.

Some of the drovers were secretly afraid of the great beasts that swung their heads and bawled and moved with such sudden speed. Others grew strangely excited, and one man foamed at the mouth. From time to time one of the drovers made a mistake, driving the cattle in the wrong direction, while others tried to turn them back. Then the bullocks jostled and fought, bruising themselves on the iron railings of the stalls, and staining themselves with their own dung and urine as they skidded on the wet slimy concrete. Each drover carried a stick, which he wielded at every opportunity. One, who had broken his stick, swung a length of plastic hosepipe.

At long last the pandemonium died away, and, unmolested, the bullocks stood quietly in their stalls. Each was marked on either flank with a blob of sticky grease, to which was stuck its lot number. As the sale began, each bullock passed in turn on to a weighing machine, so that all present at the auction could see how much meat they were buying. In the ring the farmer stood with his beasts, and as each bullock was sold it was caught by the head in an iron clamp. Then, to eliminate any chance of its being sold twice, its ear was punched, and a ring of cartilage cut from the living flesh. Now the floors of the pens were spattered with blood.

Again the bullocks waited, trembling after their ordeal, and again they were herded into trucks and driven to the abattoirs. Here they passed the long night, watered, but without food, seeking what solace they could from each other's company. At dawn they assisted their butchers for the last time, by walking up the long ramp to their death. They went willingly, still seeking wide skies and the sunshine.

Duncan stood in the straw-covered ring, one of his beasts by his side. He was pleasurably surprised. Both animals just topped the half ton mark, so he would not lose so much on the sale as he had expected. Above him he heard the monotonous voice of the auctioneer, as he exhorted the assembled butchers to bid. "Come along now, gentlemen. Best bit of baby beef we've seen this morning. Who'll start us off? Who'll say ten? Ten? Nine fifteen?"

The minutes passed. A stony silence deepened. Bewildered, Duncan looked round the ring, and caught the fishlike, glassy stare of Thomas Redd as he leaned against the rails. No one was looking at the auctioneer. They were all staring coldly at him. Suddenly, with a sick chill of anger and disgust, he realized that no one was going to bid. He turned to the auctioneer. "Withdraw them from the sale," he snapped and, face aflame, he strode from the ring.

Back at the farm, Duncan broke the news to Marjorie. "Now I know what it's like to be hunted," he said wearily. "You expected this, didn't you? You knew this was going to happen."

Marjorie nodded and said nothing. She felt near to tears at the way Duncan was being treated, and at Duncan's unspoken thought—that these were her people, that she was one one of them, and he was the outsider.

"You were right," said Duncan. "I should have taken them farther afield." Then he grinned. "Floury will just have to wait for his money now. At least they can't do much else to us."

Here, however, Duncan was wrong. He had forgotten that Penny was still vulnerable.

It was Jago who started it, Jago and Martin and the Purley boys. They danced around Penny as she stood in the school playground on her first day back at school. "Us've got a new game, Penny. We're the Hunt."

"I don't want to play," said Penny coldly.

"Yes you do," said Jago. "You've got to, because we're the Hunt, and you're the hind. You're a girt old hind that's been stealing apples in farmer Feather's orchard, and we're going to run you down and cut you open, and eat the apples as they fall to the ground."

"Go away," Penny cried. "You're foul, and I shan't play. I shan't run."

"Yes you will." Martin laughed. "Cos us'll put the tufters in and rouse 'ee and set 'ee afoot. Come on lads."

They went too far, and her cries of fear quickly turned to shrill screams of pain, screams that met the ears of the games mistress as she sauntered into the playground on a routine check. Five minutes later, white faced and feeling slightly sick, she was knocking on the door of the headmaster's study. "One for you, Head, I think."

Swiftly she outlined what had been happening. "I thought I knew these little beasts, but apparently I've still got a lot to learn. Penny's black and blue. Her thighs and buttocks are covered with pinch marks, and the skin is broken in several places. They might have killed her."

"Possessed by the devil," murmured the head. "A spot of swift exorcism is called for, I think." He went to the cupboard, and after rummaging around for a moment drew out a long, thin cane. He swished it through the air. "It's a long time since I used this. I hope it's still in good condition."

The games mistress eyed it doubtfully. "Are you sure?" she asked. "Isn't corporal punishment frowned upon nowadays?"

"We're wasting time," snapped the headmaster. "Wheel them in."

He waited in the silence of the study. If he was wrong in this instance, then he didn't want to be a teacher any longer. He had seen this sort of thing before. Every so often a deep primeval instinct came bubbling up from the slime of the subconscious, turning a normal indi-

141

vidual into the mindless unit of a pack. It was useless to try to destroy or eradicate this trait. One could only hope to drive it back, deep down, and restore the mind to sanity by pain. The pain would linger, as a reminder of the dangers of giving way to such instincts.

He surveyed the ragged uncomfortable line that stood before him. Already they were beginning to feel the first twinges of remorse and shame at what they had done. "Hunting, eh?" murmured the Head. "You were the hounds, and Penny the hind. Now I'm going to play. I'm the whipper-in."

They knew what was coming, but they were totally unprepared for the cold ferocity of their punishment. Afterward, tearful and trembling, they filed out of the study into the corridor. At first Jago was defiant. "He can't do this to us anymore. Wait till I get home and see my dad."

The others demurred. "He served us bad, and he could do it again. Us don't want no more of that kind of treatment. You bide quiet, Jago, or it will be worse for you."

Without needing much persuasion, Jago gave in. His words of defiance had been no more than a token show of bravado. More imaginative than the rest, he had suddenly seen himself as if from afar, caught in the act of tormenting Penny. He felt sickened and ashamed. He realized that he liked the little girl. His shoulders crumpled and he began to sob, but he was not sorry for himself. He wept for Penny.

Marjorie also wept, but that was while she was alone, as Penny slept in the little white bedroom at the back of the house. When Duncan came in from the lambing fields, cold and weary and smelling of sheep, she was composed and ready for him. Coldly, she told him what had happened, and as the rage began to well up inside him, she quenched it, as effectively as she would douse a candle flame.

"Before you blame anyone else, look at yourself, and ask yourself how much you are to blame. Ask yourself, what are you doing, and why? You're not concerned with Penny anymore, or me. You don't care what happens. All that matters is your stubborn pride, your determination that these people won't get you down. You're asking to be punished more and more, just so you can pretend it doesn't hurt."

Duncan stood looking at her, and his face was that of a stranger, wooden, unheeding. "Is there anything to eat? If not I'll get going. I've a lot to do this afternoon."

With an effort, Marjorie controlled her anger. She put her hands on Duncan's shoulders, forcing him to look down at her. "Duncan, please, hear me out. You knew, when we took this farm, that hunting was a way of life here." She stopped for a moment. "Do you remember that night, before Penny was born, when we drove round the corner and found the car crash?"

Duncan shuddered involuntarily. Over the years, the image came back, as vividly as if it had just happened, the stabbing headlights, the man leaning drunkenly against the car, his face split in an obscene red grin, and his jaw hanging loose, the woman, white and blank of face, nursing a baby.

Marjorie was speaking, softly. "Supposing Penny had

143

seen that? Wouldn't that have been just as horrible for her? Would you have tried to get all cars banned because of it? Penny was upset at what she saw, not so much because a hind was killed, but because she thought the hind was Kit. It's no good trying to change the circumstances of our life if in so doing we destroy ourselves. That's what you're doing now, Duncan. You're destroying us, Penny and me."

She began to cry, softly, her head pressed against his chest and her hands gripping his shoulders. Gently, he guided her to the sofa and they sat down. "Give me time to think," he begged. "An hour or two, and then I'll let you know."

"No, Duncan. You've had plenty of time. You've lost. You never had a chance. If deer hunting does die out, it will be because of a change in the people who now hunt and who support the Hunt. Nothing you can do, no sacrifice you make, will bring about this change. It must come from within the people themselves."

She stood up and swiftly dried her eyes. "Go out now, remove those silly signs, and by tomorrow this will seem like a bad dream. It will be as if it never happened, and people will be just the same as before. Ted was right, and he tried to warn you."

Duncan sat staring at the fire, his fingers absently plucking at a small tear in the sofa. "And if I don't?" he queried.

"Then first thing tomorrow morning I'm taking Penny and going to stay with Pauline and Mike in South Devon. I've had just about as much as I can take, and I know Penny has. You must please yourself."

15

The Dark Heritage

The morning was gray and mild with the false promise of spring. A thrush sang in the ash tree, but Duncan's heart was heavy as he loaded the suitcases into the back of the car. A mood of bleak depression that had come over him after his public humiliation in the auction ring had steadily deepened so that now he scarcely heeded Marjorie as she bade him good-bye.

In the days that followed he wandered about the farm, perfunctorily carrying out such tasks as were necessary for the well-being of his stock. The rest of his work he neglected, and at night he sat brooding in the empty, deserted house. Short of total surrender, he could see no way out of the situation, and although his wife and child had left him, he was still convinced that what he had done was for Penny's sake. He failed to see that what Marjorie had done was also in the child's interests.

On the afternoon of the fifth day he stood alone, watching the sunlight as it slanted through the window. The rays shone dully on the twin blue barrels of the shotgun that hung in the rafters. Almost dreamily, Duncan took it down from the nails. Gently, he stroked the polished walnut stock and then moved to the cupboard where the cartridges were kept. He put his hand in the box, then checked himself, shaking his head absent-mindedly. He had taken a handful of cartridges. This time he needed only one.

Outside the air was clean and cold. He walked into the sun, taking the rough green track that led over the hill. Behind him storm clouds massed in purple array over the rounded hills. The fields in the valley were vivid green, dotted with white clusters of sheep. He sat down and looked out, across the valley to where the oak woods stood black against the sunset, and as he watched, he saw the tall deer moving across the brow of the hill. They stopped, and one, a ten pointer, stood with his mane and antlers aflame with gold from the sun.

An hour later Duncan still sat on the hill, and it seemed to him that the friendship of the night was the one solace left to him in an alien world. His course of action, which had seemed so clear cut, so sensible a way out when he had left the farmhouse, he now saw to be an illusion, shattered into a thousand fragments by the doubts that assailed his mind. If he were to destroy himself now, it would mean that he denied that life had any meaning or pattern at all, that everything that had happened had been merely a hideous waste of time.

He still wanted to put the barrel of the gun to his head, to pull the trigger and find oblivion, but he saw that, just as he had accepted the joys of life without question, assuming them to be his rightful heritage, he now had to endure the dark side of life. He who abhorred the taking of life had to spare his own, to live with the knowledge that he had tried and failed.

He knew of only one man he felt he could talk to. Still carrying the gun, he got up and set off through the darkness.

Isaac stood at the door of his cottage, his vast bulk blocking the yellow glare of the light, and looked at the drawn white face of the man with the gun. "Come in," he said, and Duncan followed him into the room.

Isaac held out his hand, without comment, and Duncan handed over the gun. Snapping open the breech, Isaac extracted the single cartridge. He stood the gun in a corner and motioned to Duncan to sit down. Then he poured a generous measure of clear liquid from a dark bottle and handed it over without a word. Duncan drank, gasping as the fiery liquid bit at his throat. The warmth spread down into his stomach, and Duncan wondered what it was, guessing it was something the old man brewed himself.

Isaac jerked his head at the shotgun in the corner. "You came pretty close to it then," he said.

Duncan nodded, and gave a brief sigh. "At the time,

it seemed the most sensible thing to do. Now I'm not so sure."

Isaac poured himself a drink and sat down before the fire, spreading his legs to the blaze. "There's many a man before you reasoned his way into a crazy situation. For once, though, you must have listened to your heart instead of your head."

"I should have listened to it a long time ago," muttered Duncan, staring at the fire.

"Aye," agreed Isaac. "But then, hindsight is the bitter truth we have to swallow, the price we pay for having the impudence to imagine we possess foresight. We have lost the power to foresee and forestall, if indeed we were ever endowed with it, except in a limited and groping way. That's why we tend to destroy ourselves."

The fire was burning low. Carefully, Isaac heaped fresh logs upon the embers, arranging them with expert skill, so that the yellow flames leapt and crackled. "The stored sunlight of centuries," the old man murmured, "squandered for the sake of a few moments' warmth." He squinted up from the hearth, his eyes sparked with flickering light. "Tell me," he asked. "What went wrong?"

Dully, Duncan told him the whole story, the finding of Kit, his enmity with the Hunt, his public humiliation, and the persecution of his daughter. Toward the end his voice faltered, almost breaking as he spoke of the depression that had led him to the verge of suicide.

Isaac listened, his face a mask, his drink forgotten in his glass, and after Duncan had finished he sat for a long time, apparently deep in thought. In reality he was fight-

ing the eruption of a rage that threatened to consume him, to drive him out to rend and tear and destroy until he had avenged the wrongs that had been done to this man. Once he had killed a man in such a fury, breaking his body with his bare hands. The secret was locked within him, for no one suspected that the battered body found at the foot of the cliffs had met his death other than accidentally. Since then Isaac had learned to control his anger.

Duncan's glass was empty. Isaac replenished it, then drained and refilled his own. Right now, he considered, the important thing was to snap Duncan out of his depression and misery, and the easiest way to do that was to rekindle the fires of wrath that had threatened to consume Duncan and which still smoldered just beneath the surface. It was a risk, for Duncan was now a desperate man, and his violence, once roused, might become uncontrollable. Isaac decided to draw the flames upon himself.

"You made two big mistakes, didn't you?" he said coldly. "Oh, you're not the first, by a long chalk, and I'm thinking you won't be the last, but I'm hoping you can learn from them. Your first mistake was in using your moral principles as props to support your personal vendetta against the Hunt. There's nothing wrong with your beliefs. They're sound, but they started to corrode when they came in contact with your bitterness and your hate. Your second mistake was that you forgot to forgive."

As Isaac anticipated, Duncan leapt to his feet. His face was white and he was trembling with cold anger. "I'll be on my way," he said. "I didn't come here to listen to you preaching forgiveness."

"You aren't going anywhere," said Isaac softly. "I didn't invite you here, but I paid you the courtesy of hearing your story. Now repay me by listening while I speak."

Duncan hesitated. Isaac barred his way, and Duncan knew that the old man could pick him up with one hand and smash him against the wall like a toy. He subsided into his chair with a sigh.

Isaac waved his hand to the uncurtained window, to where yellow lamp light flooded the side of the hill. "What do you see out there?"

"Why nothing," answered Duncan. "Only darkness, and the wild daffodils nodding in the wind."

"Aye, daffodils," said Isaac. "Nodding. They bend and they sway in the wind of adversity and so they survive. If they were rigid, unbending, they'd snap. Forgiving is like bending. I have my creed, and I share my beliefs whether people want to hear them or not." He chuckled. "At least I make them listen, but I have no right to insist that others accept my beliefs. If they refuse, I can only forgive, and ask forgiveness, for only then can I try again. The alternative is destruction."

"Aren't we all bent on a course of destruction?" asked Duncan. "Try as I might, I can see no point or purpose in this existence of ours, or any hope of changing it." He stared out into the night, at the windblown grass and the flowers that glowed like pale torches on their green stems. "Sometimes I wonder," he said, half to himself. "Who are we? And where are we going?"

Isaac sat back, his head sunk on his chest and his shaggy brows lowered so that his eyes were sunk in shadow. "I know that before I was born I was at one with my environment. I was a shoal of mackerel swimming in the sea. I was an ear of wheat in a field of grain, the soil beneath an oak. I came from the soil, and I will return there. I ask nothing more than that I shall lie alone upon some forgotten hill and that the grasses shall flower among my bones. It would be presumptuous of me to imagine that my life is in any way more detached or remote from my environment than my state before birth, or after death. I don't know where my earthly body ends or my soul begins. I don't even know the bounds of my environment. It begins somewhere inside me, and stretches far beyond the horizon. Body and soul, I am inseparable from it."

He looked across at Duncan. It seemed to him that the man was calmer, more at peace. His eyes were clearer, and he seemed to be watching for something, as yet far distant. Isaac spoke again. "I find this difficult to put into words, without giving the wrong impression, without implying a world of unbridled license, but I live for a life when everyone is free, when people do exactly what they want to do, secure in the happiness that their actions are guiltless, that they can do no wrong, simply because they do not want to sin. Freedom from guilt, it's the only true freedom. All the rest are false."

For a long time there was silence, broken only by the crackle of the fire. "What am I to do?" asked Duncan.

"You could try getting drunk," said Isaac. "I don't recommend it. I tried it, and for a while it worked. I found oblivion. But now the more I drink the more my mind bubbles and ferments, like some bewitched cauldron. It's not the bright nightmares on the surface that I mind now, but the shadowy truths that writhe like eels in the obscure murk of the depths. These are what I fear. You could try entering a monastery. It's no way to live, but a wonderful way to die. But then, you've rejected death as a solution. Why not emigrate?"

"You mean . . . run away?" asked Duncan.

Isaac gave a mighty shout of laughter. "I would hesitate to suggest to the inhabitants of Australia or New Zealand that they were a bunch of cowards. Look at it this way. There's nothing for you here. Only the dust of past regrets. And I think you'll fit better with people who are more progressive, less shackled by the chains of ancient and binding traditions. As for you running away, well, you changed your mind about that earlier this evening. Wherever you go, you have to live with yourself."

"But what about the Hunt and my farm?" asked Duncan. "Is everything I have endured, all that my family have suffered, to be in vain?"

"Leave that to me," said Isaac. "I have an idea. I don't want to say any more about it at the moment, but don't be surprised if you have visitors in the next few days. Just trust me, and meantime have a talk with Marjorie. I'm sure she will fall in with your plans. That is, of course, if you've decided to take my advice."

Duncan stood up, and for the first time that evening he smiled. "I think I have. I'll go now, and thank you."

Isaac picked up the gun and held it out to him. Duncan took it hesitantly and ran his finger over the smooth, worn stock. "I shan't need it again," he said. "Would you like it?"

Isaac shook his head. "Like you, I long ago learned the futility of killing."

He saw Duncan to the door and watched as the darkness swallowed him up. For a long time he stood on the step, walking in spirit with Duncan through the velvet softness of the night. He remembered the words of a writer who lived not far away. Although now an old man, the writer's mind was still razor sharp, his perception as keen as the eye of a hawk. He too had loved Exmoor and the tall red deer. What was it Henry Williamson had written? "All the misery in the human world has been caused by a lack of imaginative understanding."

Isaac sighed. For how many years had that thought rung true, and for how long would people remain deaf to its tone?

16

The Sale of Slade Farm

Rather dubiously, Duncan wrote to Marjorie, suggesting that they should sell the farm and emigrate, and to his surprise and delight received a reply by return mail. Marjorie was enthusiastic about the idea and announced her intention of returning as soon as she could, so that together they could make plans and prepare the farm for sale. Feeling happier than he had been for some time, Duncan set to work, cleaning the farmhouse and attending to all the tasks he had neglected of late.

At dusk of the same day, he heard the sound of an approaching car. Scarcely able to believe that Marjorie could be returning so soon, yet filled with sudden hope, he rushed to the door. The car was unfamiliar to him, and his spirits fell as he watched the two occupants get out. Then his interest quickened as he recognized one of the men as Adamson, the man who had shot the lame old hind that had robbed him of his oats.

The other man was past middle age, thin and pale, looking strangely out of place in his dark city clothes as he picked his way carefully across the yard, a bulging briefcase tucked under one bony arm. Adamson introduced him, "This is Mr. Moss, Mr. Turner. Mr. Moss has a little proposition to put to you, if you can spare a few minutes of your time."

Puzzled, Duncan invited them in, but Adamson declined. "I'll take a stroll, if you don't mind. I could do with some fresh air, so I'll leave you and Mr. Moss to talk in private for a while." With a smile and a wave he was gone, leaving Duncan and the stranger standing on the doorstep.

Duncan led the way into the house and motioned to Mr. Moss to sit down. The man had a curious, birdlike air about him, partly because of his careful way of walking, and partly from his habit of jerking his head on the end of his long neck and peering intently from side to side. Now he sat, his briefcase resting on his knees and his hands folded above it, looking, thought Duncan, like a roosting fowl.

"Mr. Adamson tells me that he has heard from a reliable source that you are thinking of selling this property."

Straight to the point, thought Duncan. Isaac hadn't wasted any time. This must be the visitor he was warned to expect. Aloud he said, "My wife and I have discussed the idea, but nothing is decided as yet, and we certainly haven't put the property on the market."

"Supposing you did decide to sell," said Mr. Moss. "How do you propose to go about it?"

Duncan shrugged. "By auction I suppose, unless it was sold by private treaty beforehand."

Mr. Moss nodded. "I am in a position to save you a considerable amount of trouble and expense. I have been instructed to offer you fifteen percent of the total value of your property above the price agreed by independent valuation. Lock, stock, and barrel, Mr. Turner. All you need do is accept the check, hand over the key, and walk out. In your own time, of course. We are in no hurry to take possession."

For a few moments Duncan sat speechless. "Fifteen percent," he echoed. "But you haven't even seen the place yet. Who are you? Whose money are you throwing about?"

Mr. Moss sighed patiently. "Let me explain. I represent the League for the Abolition of Blood Sports. No doubt you have heard of our organization."

Duncan nodded. "For some time," continued Mr. Moss, "we have tried unsuccessfully to get stag hunting banned by law. No doubt we shall succeed one day, but meantime many animals are being caused needless suffering. We have therefore decided to buy as much property as we can obtain in this area, as and when it becomes available, and so create sanctuaries, or harbors, for the deer, where the Hunt dare not trespass. If we cannot get stag hunting banned, we can at least make it more difficult to hunt. As for throwing money about, we are offering you a very good price. We realize this, and once the sale has been successfully negotiated, we intend to make the fact known. This need cause you no embarrassment whatever, and we hope it will encourage others to sell."

He stood up and walked over to the window, where he stood looking out over the valley. "Obviously the state of the premises does not interest us. It is the locality that is of importance. If you do not feel our offer to be a fair one, put the property up for auction. In the long run you might not find yourself so well off, and the chances are we shall have bought the place anyway, because our agents will be bidding in secret. We are prepared to take that gamble, but you will have had a lot of work for nothing."

Duncan sat silent, thinking hard. Mr. Moss spoke again, his voice soft and persuasive. "There's another way of looking at this, one which I feel sure will appeal to a man of your sentiments. Not only are you realizing your capital and saving yourself trouble, but you will leave behind a sanctuary, a haven, for all the wild creatures for which, in the past, you have expressed concern."

Suddenly, Duncan made up his mind. Rising to his feet, he held out his hand. "Congratulations, Mr. Moss. You've just bought yourself a farm."

From then on events moved rapidly. In spite of Mr. Moss's bland assurances, there was still a great deal to do, but Marjorie, once she had recovered from the shock of having her home sold from beneath her feet, worked willingly, attending to a hundred and one details, all of which had to be arranged, but had not even entered Duncan's head.

At last the day came when, one fine summer's morning, they stood in silence, looking for the last time at the little house that had been their home. The lilac was in bloom, and the bees were busy among the massed blossoms of mauve and white. The air was filled with the scents and sounds of the English countryside, and for a moment Duncan was swept by a great wave of panic, coupled with an overwhelming desire to put back the clock, to restore his life to the old familiar pattern. Beside him Marjorie stifled a sob, and he laid his hand on her shoulder. Resolutely he led her to the car where Penny was waiting, and they drove away without looking back.

The League for the Abolition of Blood Sports had installed a warden at the farm who, for the preceding week, had lived with Duncan and Marjorie, gradually taking over the running of the place. Alistair Cameron was a burly, bearded young man, a shepherd from the lowland hills of Scotland. Dour, uncommunicative, well used to a solitary existence, it seemed improbable that he would have any contact with the local people, let alone be influenced by them. His job would be gradually to run down the livestock on the farm and to grow crops that would supplement the diet of the deer on the hills. He was quite confident that he could handle any situation that might arise.

Soon after the Turners left, the disturbances began. At first the incidents were trivial, a gate torn from its hinges and thrown aside, so that the stock strayed, a faucet in the yard turned on during the night, sending precious gallons of water to waste, and turning the yard into a muddy quagmire. Alistair shrugged and carried on his work as normal. He had been warned to expect trouble of this kind, but he was well able to take care of himself, and he had no wife or children to worry about.

Then came the dark of the moon, when the nights were still and calm, lit only by the wan light of the stars. Alistair was wakened from sleep by a thunderous knocking at the door. Grumbling a little, he grabbed a flashlight and made his way downstairs, wondering who it could be whose business was so urgent that they should come calling at this hour of night.

There was no one there. Alistair stood on the step, shivering in the cold air, his anger rising as he shone his flashlight into the shadowy corners of the yard. Next moment there came the splintering crash of breaking glass. It came from the back of the house, and cursing, Alistair raced in the direction of the sound, his heavy flashlight upraised and ready to use as a weapon on any intruder.

There was nothing, only the shattered spears of glass, and a stone lying on the floor. Slowly, Alistair walked back to the door and went outside. "Come out," he bellowed into the darkness. "Come out, wherever you are, and let's see what you are made of. I'm ready for you."

The minutes passed, and Alistair waited, his anger cooling as he stood listening in the silence. At long last he turned on his heel and went indoors. As he shot home the bolts he heard a splintering thud as a heavy stone pitched against the door. His hair prickled on the back of his neck as he realized that whoever had thrown the stone must have been watching out there in the night and could just as easily have hit him with it as he had turned to enter the house. Alistair decided it was time to have a word with the police.

Next morning he found his truck wrecked, its tires slashed and the engine choked with sand. Grimly he tramped off into town. The police sergeant was sympathetic but unhelpful. "Even if you had the telephone, Mr. Cameron, it would be twenty minutes or more before we could reach you, and then it would probably be too late. The intruders could be miles away by then. We just haven't enough men to mount a constant watch, but we will get a patrol car to check round now and again. From what you tell me, it doesn't sound as though they mean to cause you any physical harm."

"Thanks a lot," said Alistair sardonically. "I hope you are right. I would hate to prove you wrong."

There would be nights when nothing happened to disturb the peace, but frequently Alistair would awake and lie listening, wondering what was happening outside. He never caught sight of his enemies, and sometimes he did not even hear them, but next morning he would find evidence of their visit. Once his letterbox, which also served as a container for his deliveries of bread and milk, was besmirched and defiled so that it was no longer usable. His chicken house was overturned and the fowls slaughtered. Any vegetables he tried to grow were torn from the ground.

On several occasions he tried waiting up, lying in ambush with a shotgun, but he couldn't stay awake indefinitely. Sleep was difficult enough at the best of times, for he never knew when he was likely to be awakened by lights flashing on the windows, to lie listening to stealthy footsteps or the sound of mocking laughter. Once he fired out of the window, ducking back hurriedly as echoing shots rang out of the darkness and a hail of pellets rattled on the roof.

He grew weary and dispirited. Several times he reported his plight to his employers, but although the league promised to send help, no one arrived.

One morning early in September he noticed that the water tasted strange. Turning on the faucet in the kitchen, he let the water run swirling into the sink. It was faintly cloudy and discolored, and as he watched he saw to his disgust that several fat white maggots had come out of the faucet. Leaving the house, he climbed the hill to the spring that supplied the water, and there in the tank he found a pig, its features frozen by death into a derisory grin, its bloated corpse seething with maggots that one by one fell off into the water.

It was the last straw. That morning he packed and left, sending a curt note of resignation, together with the keys of the farm, to the head office of the League for the Abolition of Blood Sports.

The league did not bother to replace him. The stock had long since been disposed of, and now the farm stood empty and deserted in the dying sun of summer. The chimney grew cold, and the house seemed to shrink into the earth, as gradually, the wild began to reclaim its own.

17

Return to the Hills

Rhus was returning north. Three winters had passed since the beginning of his exile, and during that time he had grown and matured so that in weight and size he far exceeded any other stag. His antlers, massive in spread and width of beam, were ample proof of the years of rich living, for in addition to carrying the brow, bay, and trey tines, his left antler had four points on top, while his right bore five.

He had passed the summer peacefully by the wooded banks of a broad salmon river, loitering undisturbed in the green shade of the trees. Then came a morning when the spiders' webs shimmered silver in the dew, and the blackberries shone like dark stars in the hedgerows. During that day Rhus began to shake and tremble with the first fevers of the rut, and he prowled moodily through the woods, grunting softly to himself and pausing to slash angrily at any small tree or bush that came within his vision.

With the coming of the night the skies clouded, and a moist wind shook the oaks, battering down from the north and tearing leaves and twigs from the swaying branches. The air was strong with the scent of the sea and the heather-clad moors, and Rhus set his face to the wind, moving purposefully through the darkness.

By dawn he had covered thirty miles. The gale had blown itself out, and as the first pale rays of the sun lit the storm-washed landscape, Rhus took shelter in a small copse, close by a sunken lane. His arrival disturbed a fox, who had also thought to pass the day in the security of the wood. Because of the storm, the fox had failed to make a kill during the night, so that in addition to being cold and wet, he was hungry.

The fox had no wish to challenge the mighty strength of the stag, and so, reluctantly, he abandoned his couch in the fern. He did not move far, but lay, morose and wakeful, in the ditch beside the lane. An hour passed, and Rhus dozed, his head drooping under the weight of his antlers, but the fox remained alert, hoping he could return to the wood. His pointed muzzle rested lightly on his outstretched forepaws, and his thick brush lay curled against his flanks. Although he seemed relaxed, he was ready for instant movement, should the occasion arise.

Soft-footed over the sodden grass that carpeted the

lane, a boy approached, the weight of a shotgun heavy under his arm, the dark steel of the barrels cold to his hand. He was heading for the copse, in the hope that rabbits would be feeding in the early light.

Fox and boy heard the soft clucking of the moorhen as it strode nervously up the lane, the white bars of its tail flashing and the red of its bill nodding as it looked for worms and insects in the grass. The boy froze in the shadow of the hedge, hoping that the bird would not be panicked into a sudden noisy flight that might scare the rabbits. The fox tensed for a spring as hunger returned and his jaws ran with saliva.

While the boy watched, the moorhen seemed to freeze, as for a brief second the springing fox hung in midair, his mouth open and his bushy tail streaming behind him. Then the fox was down, feet asprawl, and the white teeth closed in an audible snap, but already the moorhen was on the move, its wings flapping and its legs jerking as it struggled to fly. The jaws of the fox closed on its tail, and the bird pulled free, leaving the killer to shake the feathers from his mouth.

For a moment it seemed that the moorhen would escape, and it was already airborne, flying two feet off the ground as the fox struck again, leaping high into the air and snapping at the flapping wing. Then the bird was down, and the fox had it by the head.

Throughout the whole of this drama the boy had watched, spellbound, the gun on his arm forgotten. Only when the fox gathered the palpitating remains of the moorhen in his jaws and turned to leap the hedge did the boy remember that the fox was the farmer's enemy, the killer of poultry and lambs. His shot blew the fox from its feet, and woke Rhus to instant flight.

The bulk of the stag seemed to fill the lane, and his antlers whipped the overhanging branches as his hooves drummed the earth. The boy fell backward into the hedge, the second barrel of his gun discharging harmlessly into the air, and before he could collect his wits sufficiently to reload, Rhus was gone, his powerful hindquarters thrusting him forward in a series of great bounding leaps. Cursing and trembling, the boy collected the body of the fox that had robbed him of the greater prize and made his way slowly home.

Rhus passed an uneasy day hidden in a field of kale. He lay flat, his neck outstretched so that his antlers were spread horizontally across his neck and back. When, occasionally, he raised his head to listen, or shake off the flies that plagued him, his antlers showed above the green growing stems of kale, but although a road bordered the field, and many people passed by, none was observant enough to spot him.

Dusk came, and with it a resurgence of the restlessness that drove Rhus on. As the mist stole out of the valleys, and the quavering hoot of an owl echoed across the stubble fields, Rhus left the kale. The moon rose on his right, winging sickle shaped over the dark backcloth of the sky, and as the planets moved, each in its appointed orbit, Rhus journeyed over darkened fields, through wood and copse, crossing hills and valleys in his long trek north.

All around him the world of man lay sleeping. Once, as he crossed a lonely road, he was caught for a brief instant in the white glare of a car's headlights. A dog barked as he skirted a farmhouse, and a hunting otter whickered and bared his teeth as he crossed a stream. The hills grew steeper, their slopes clad in dense woodland, and the white water foamed among the stones of the riverbeds. As the stars paled, and a faint aura of light mirrored the eastern sky, Rhus stood alone on a heather-clad hill. Below him the oakwoods lay spread like a shaggy cloak, and beyond stretched the Severn sea, with the lights of Wales shining through the mist. Rhus lifted his head to greet the dawn, and from his throat came the deep rumbling, bellowing roar of the rutting stag.

Far away, like an echo from the distant hills, there came an answering call. Rhus listened, and then gave voice to his challenge once more, stretching his neck and lowering his head so that the sound boomed out over the heather, sending a flock of sheep scuttling away in nervous panic. Then, as the response came again, he set off in the direction of the call. He grunted savagely as he trotted over the wiry heather, his muscles rippling under his red hide.

The two stags met on level ground. They circled warily, slow, catlike, each trying to intimidate the other with a display of broad, gleaming flank, shaggy mane, and white, rolling eye. Rhus was bigger and heavier than his opponent, but the other stag was an experienced warrior, victor of many a joust, and skilled in the use of his deadly brow tines.

He came in fast, his attack so sudden and unexpected that it caught Rhus unprepared. Somehow he got his antlers down in time to parry the other's thrust, but the shock of the impact threw him back so that he sat in an undignified heap on the turf. Instantly, he recovered, and in an explosion of anger he fought back, shaking his head until the other lost his grip. As he broke away Rhus scored, his brow tine cutting a red furrow deep in the other's shoulder.

The two stags reared high in the air, their hooves chopping down, cutting at face and neck and chest. Then their antlers locked together in a splintering crash, and the minutes passed as they stood straining, their eyes rolling and their breath coming in great sobs. Gradually Rhus's superior strength overcame his opponent. Slowly, remorselessly, he forced the other stag backward, across the clearing, to the edge of the steep combe. Suddenly it was all over, and Rhus stood triumphant as the vanquished stag half fell, half rolled downhill into a tangle of gorse and fern.

The small group of hinds that had watched the combat now began to feed, cropping the short, sheep-bitten turf that grew at their feet, all, save one, oblivious to their new master. This hind had felt excitement growing within her while the battle raged, and now she moved closer to Rhus as he rolled on the ground, scoring the turf with his antlers.

Rhus scrambled to his feet, his nostrils flaring as the hind rubbed herself against his flanks. She turned away, and he followed, eager to possess her. Then for a brief moment it seemed the skies darkened and the ground shook in the explosion of their mating.

That evening, the hind led Rhus and the herd down off the moors, through the woods, and into the farmland in the valley. Rhus followed closely, fearful lest one of the hinds should stray too far and be appropriated by a rival stag. There were seven hinds in the herd, and Rhus had to be continually on the alert. From time to time he roared his challenge, and younger stags, hearing the deep note of authority, wisely kept their distance. They remained in attendance, however, skulking in the shadows among the trees, ever watchful, ever alert, each knowing instinctively that one day the champion would fall, worn out by his own exertions and vigilance.

The farmland Rhus and his herd skirted was in ruins, the fields dirty and unkempt. After Alistair Cameron had been driven away by the persecution of hooligans and would-be poachers, the League for the Abolition of Blood Sports had allowed the farm to lie derelict. From time to time a contractor came and made a few halfhearted attempts to till the land, but he never stayed more than a few hours, and always left before night-fall. For most of the time the farm was deserted.

Farmer Feather was loud in his complaints against the League. His land bordered Slade Farm, and he claimed that deer broke into his fields, stealing his crops and spoiling his hedges, allowing his stock to stray. Secretly he encouraged his bullocks to wander onto Slade Farm and made sure they could feed at night on the few crops sown for the deer. The woods became the haunt of poachers, setting snares and shooting any game they came across.

Only the Hunt stayed away, for Baskerville had no wish to suffer adverse publicity or to run the risk of prosecution for trespass should hounds stray on to the land owned by the League. The Hunt no longer met in that part of the moor, and the farmers grumbled, but Baskerville paid no heed, knowing that the anger of the farmers was directed, not against him, but against the League.

The deer came and went as they pleased. From time to time one was shot, and several suffered gunshot wounds from which they eventually recovered. Others were caught in snares, eventually to die of slow strangulation, but one or two broke free and wore the raw red rings where the wire had cut into their hides.

The hind which had once been called Kit had never strayed far from the farm on which she had been reared, for though she had severed her ties with the humans who had lived there, she still felt an affinity for the land. In the overgrown orchard the apples were heavy on the moss-rotten branches of the trees. Here she led the herd to browse, and later to sleep in the yellow, seeding grass.

18

Uneasy Sanctuary

Throughout the season of the rut, Rhus remained invincible. His strength and vigor seemed inexhaustible. He harried his harem of hinds relentlessly, circling the herd and driving back any female who attempted to stray. Few stags dared to challenge him, and those who did were soon defeated, sent away bruised and battered into the sheltering oaks. Before long he commanded a herd of fifteen hinds, five of which had yearling calves at foot.

While the fever of the rut was on him, the days and nights were a red mist of lust and aggression. He ate and slept little, his only relief the cooling mud of the soil pit where he rolled and bathed in an effort to assuage the fires that burned within him. When the full fury of his rage possessed him, he would attack anything in sight, a branch lying on the ground, an anthill, a patch of fern. His antlers scored the earth and sent turf and soil showering over his massive shoulders, thus adding to his wild, unkempt appearance. His odor was rank, a curious scent part goat, part catlike.

For the hinds, safety lay in numbers. Such was the intensity of his strength and passion that had he singled out one hind for any length of time, he might seriously have injured her. As it was, he shared his favors equally among the herd, and so for each hind there were long periods of neglect from his attentions.

The acorns fell, and rain swept in from the Atlantic, shimmering veils of moisture that drifted over the moors, polishing each twig and stone and grass-blade, plumping the soil, and gently embedding the summer's harvest of seeds. The leaves fell, and the grasses withered and died. The summer migrants departed, the moors lay silent beneath the skies, and those creatures that were left settled down to survive yet another season of cold. It was the testing time, the period that ensured that only those best equipped to survive would live to perpetuate their kind.

Rhus was lean and haggard. Satiated, he watched the gradual dissolution of his herd without interest. He no longer belled his challenge at dusk and dawn, and even tolerated the presence of a younger stag in the company of the few remaining hinds. By the time the first snows fell the two stags were alone together, peacefully coexisting as they shared the hanging tendrils of ivy in the woodlands or scraped the snow away from the turnips in the fields.

The presence of Rhus in the district did not go unnoticed for long. Isaac came upon his slots in the snow and followed them, wondering at the size of a stag that could leave tracks longer and broader than any he had seen in a lifetime of association with red deer. The tracks led into the wood at Slade Farm, and in the gathering dusk Isaac spotted the big stag as he stampeded away over the frozen ground. One glimpse was enough to convince Isaac that Slade Farm harbored a stag finer than had been seen in the area for many a year. He kept the knowledge secret, but others must have seen Rhus as well, for in the Wheatsheaf there was gossip about a "girt old stag with a head like a hatrack."

Isaac heard the rumors and was deeply troubled. For some time he had worried about the poaching he knew was going on at Slade Farm, but he had not known what to do. The League seemed content merely to keep the land as a barrier to the Hunt, rather than to manage it as a proper sanctuary, and only when the Hunt met anywhere near did the League have patrols out, in the hope of catching the Hunt trespassing.

Now it seemed to Isaac that it was only a question of time before someone, more greedy or reckless than the others, took a shot at the big stag. Isaac decided that the time had come when the poaching had to stop, and if no one else would guard the sanctuary, he would. He felt he owed it to Duncan Turner.

In the days that followed he began to keep watch,

moving softly through the leafless oaks, and lying in wait, especially at dusk and dawn, in the hope of surprising an intruder. High on the hill, where the wood gave way to the high moors, he found a shaggy outcrop of rock, which afforded concealment and a little shelter from the wind. Here was a natural vantage point from which to survey the broad sweep of the woodlands and the stream that divided the trees from the farm.

Here Isaac passed many patient hours. He seemed impervious to the weather, which, although the snow had gone, was raw and cold, and there was little sun. Isaac listened and watched, determined that if he caught anyone poaching he would make him an example that would be a deterrent to others. The days passed. He saw the big red stag, and he saw foxes and rabbits. Once an otter passed within three feet of where he stood by the stream. No poachers came near, but Isaac waited on, as patient and silent as the sentinel oaks.

At dusk on the evening of the fourth day Isaac heard a shot, and then two more in rapid succession. They came from the stream that bordered the wood, and Isaac moved downhill, passing silently from tree to tree, until at last he could look down on the poacher as he stood, his back to the woods, watching for pigeons as they flew in from the fields. His gun hung under one arm, and at his feet lay two pigeons, and a cock pheasant.

Even from behind Isaac recognized the man, one Bert Redd, a young layabout who had already acquired a bad reputation. He had a long record of vandalism and destruction and had served a term of imprisonment for robbery with violence. No one, thought Isaac with grim satisfaction, would care much what happened to Bert Redd, but others might learn from his misfortune. He waited, as dusk deepened among the trees.

A pigeon flew in fast and low. Bert lifted his gun. His first shot missed, but the second barrel caught the bird and it drifted to earth in a smoke cloud of gray plumes. Bert broke open his gun to reload, and at that moment Isaac dropped on him.

The force of the impact drove Bert downhill, forcing his face into the earth. Cursing, Bert twisted around to get a look at his attacker, but bony knuckles slammed into his cheek. The pain filled his eyes with tears, and next moment a dirty rag was tied over his face, blindfolding him. Bert lay still, half paralyzed, unable to breathe because of the great weight on his back. Dimly, he was aware of rough hands at work, but he was unable to resist. In a few minutes he was crucified to his own gun.

It was lashed across his shoulders, tied to his arms with tough baler twine that cut into his flesh. His elbows were bent, and his wrists strained back to the gun. The pain was agonizing, but Isaac had not finished with him yet. Bert's ankles were tied with another length of cord, so that he could hobble, but not run. The birds he had shot were hung about his neck, and then with kicks and blows he was driven to his feet.

Still blindfolded, he was herded through the wood, a nightmare journey that it seemed would never end, as he crashed into trees and tripped over fallen logs. Twigs lashed at his face and thorns tore his skin. He was bruised and battered by the stony ground, unable to protect himself as he fell. Still he was driven on, until they came to the hard surface of the road. Here Isaac abandoned him, and he wandered half-conscious until Arthur Feather, on his way to the Wheatsheaf, found him and took him to the inn.

Isaac had been at the Wheatsheaf for over an hour, quietly drinking in his accustomed place, when Arthur brought Bert in. He pretended to be as shocked and bewildered as the rest of the regulars, but in reality he was enjoying the opportunity to admire his handiwork in a good light. Bert was blubbering and cursing, his face covered in blood, his clothes hanging in rags. They had to cut him free of his bonds, and he screamed anew as they tried to return his arms to their normal position.

They poured whiskey into him, and gradually they calmed him down. He began to tell them what had happened, making up his story as he went along. He had been taking a shortcut through Slade Farm, he told them, when he was set upon by a gang. There had been at least four men, maybe more, and he hadn't stood a chance of defending himself. They had carried him to the road and dumped him, just where Arthur had found him.

The regulars in the Wheatsheaf weren't quite sure what to believe. After Bert went home they chewed the affair over, while Isaac listened in silent amusement. They guessed that Bert had been poaching on Slade Farm, but why had he been attacked? It looked like the work of a gang, because Bert was no weakling. Some-

one suggested that the League had brought in a crowd of young toughs to protect their property, but the generally agreed theory was that a gang of deer poachers from upcountry was at work, and Bert had unfortunately disturbed them. If that was the case, then Slade Farm was dangerous country, for everyone knew that professional deer poachers were ruthless men, and next time they might not stop short of killing.

At closing time Isaac returned to his cottage, well pleased with his night's work—one incurable young thug whittled down to size and used as a stern warning to others. Now there was a general fear of danger lurking at Slade Farm, and he felt confident that for a while, at least, would-be poachers would stop and ask themselves whether the odd pheasant, or even a deer, was worth the risk of getting beaten up, perhaps killed. All the same, he thought he would continue to keep an eye on the sanctuary, in case of any further trouble.

19

Baskerville States His Case

The light of early spring is bitter pale. It shines white, without warmth, and the cold is reflected in the naked silver of the ash and the polished purple of the bare birch trees that cluster like clouds upon the distant hills. Only the oaks wear a faded livery of gray green moss, fringed by a tattered veil of brown.

Spring starts slowly, with many a false promise, and though the primroses may glow like wan stars in the hedgerows, and though the wind may blow soft and warm from the south, making the thrush shout from the topmost branch of the ash, winter is still in command. But there comes a day when all is changed, when the light is burnished with the gold of the gorse. Then the dandelions glitter like new coins in the grass of the meadows, and the sky is blue. Though winter may return, with showers of stinging hail and frosts that burn and blacken the swelling buds of the ash, nothing can stem the running tide of spring.

In the golden light the two stags were as tawny as lions as they moved slowly through the wood. They had strayed a long way from the sanctuary, for the winter had been exceptionally severe, with prolonged snowfalls, followed by hard frosts. During the winter Rhus had drifted until he was close to the shores of the Severn sea, for here much of the snow had fallen as rain, and food was easier to find. Now pickings were lean, and Rhus was thankful for anything, even scraping the mold in search of a solitary acorn that had survived the winter.

Somewhere high in the leafless trees a jay screamed a sudden warning. It might have been a false alarm. The bird could have spotted an owl or been startled by a hunting stoat or fox. Sometimes, however, the harsh cry warned of the approach of dog or man, and Rhus listened, jerking his head upright. His left antler struck the bough of a tree, and fell off, landing with a clatter at his feet. The sudden loss of weight threw his head off balance, and, shaken as usual by this annual event, Rhus took off at a bound, his head held lopsided and ludicrous. Three hundred yards downhill he struck the right antler against a tree, and this too dropped off, restoring his balance, but leaving him feeling strangely lightheaded and naked. A thin trickle of blood ran from the naked stumps, oozing over his temples and cheeks, but this soon blackened and dried. The antlers lay where they had fallen, dark and twisted, indistinguishable from the countless twigs and fallen branches that littered the forest floor.

A week later, as Platt the deer harborer walked through the wood, leading his pony along the side of the hill, his foot fell upon a branch which should have snapped under his weight, but remained firm to pressure. He glanced down, and at once, as he recognized what he saw, he felt a tight knot of excitement curl inside him. He picked up the antler, wondering at the sheer weight of it, and examined the long tines. He had not seen an antler of such girth and length for many a year, and it did not need much imagination to visualize the stature of the beast that carried such an adornment. Carefully, he tethered his pony, and tied the antler to his saddle. Then, hopefully, he began to search for its twin.

Heavy rain had fallen during the week, and Platt searched in vain for any slots or signs that might indicate which way Rhus had gone. After a while he began to work in ever-increasing circles, but it grew more and more difficult for him to keep his bearings on the closely wooded hill. After more than an hour he abandoned the hopeless quest. Twice he had passed within a yard of the fallen antler, but even his sharp eyes had failed to spot it as it lay half-hidden in the withered fern.

The antler remained where it had fallen, and summer came and bracken grew dense and green around the tines. Mice gnawed the bone, and a spider spun a web around the points. Autumn came and the fern died, falling in bronze folds which were beaten down by the snow. Gradually the antler became buried, and in time it returned to the original elements from which it came.

Platt bore the other antler home and spent the evening cleaning and polishing it. As he worked he pondered, his mind twisting and turning as he considered probabilities and possibilities. Was this, he wondered, the same stag that was rumored to have spent part of the winter at Slade Farm? He guessed it probably was, for it was unlikely that two stags such as this one were at large in the district. Was it by now back at Slade Farm, or was it still near the site where he had found the antler? Platt decided to check both spots.

Other problems occupied his mind. Should he tell Baskerville and show him the antler, or should he keep his knowledge secret and hope to harbor the stag later in the year? It was too risky, he decided. Better to show Baskerville the antler, and so be the first to bring proof that such a stag existed, than to risk some farmer running to tell tales to the Master and to hint that the harborer was going about with his eyes shut. He knew that Baskerville would be at the kennels the following morning, and he made up his mind to ride over with his prize.

Platt arrived just as Baskerville, with Dick and the kennelman, had finished looking over the hounds. Now that hunting had nearly finished for the season, those hounds which were not suitable for hunting were destroyed, for there was no point in wasting meat and meal on worthless animals. The old, the lame, those who rioted and got lost, those who preferred to chase rabbits to deer, all were got rid of. "That's the list then," said

Baskerville. "Eight in all. Not too many considering. We've got a good pack together now."

"What about Warrior?" said Dick. "You didn't make up your mind. He's been a good hound, but his teeth are gone now, and I fancy he's not as fast as he used to be."

Baskerville hesitated. He was fond of old Warrior and hated to see him go. For a moment he considered taking him as a house pet, but immediately he rejected the idea. The house was full of animals already, and he doubted if Warrior would settle away from the pack. "Very well," he said shortly, "knock him on the head with the rest."

Platt wandered over and joined the group. Casually, he unwrapped the antler and handed it to Baskerville. He heard the sudden indrawn hiss of breath and saw the man's eyes narrow as he took the horn, so he was not deceived by the Master's seemingly casual comment, "Nice horn that, Platt. Did you find the other?"

Platt shook his head.

"Pity, they would have been worth something if you had." He handed the antler to Dick, who examined it carefully.

"Only a youngster," murmured the huntsman in surprise. "He should be an outstanding specimen in a couple of years' time."

"Nonsense," scoffed Baskerville. "You don't get antler growth like that in a young stag. He's eight years old if he's a day."

Dick hesitated, realizing he was treading on dangerous ground in arguing with the Master, especially in front

183

of Platt and the kennelman. "I could be wrong I suppose. It's only my opinion, but judging by the lack of pearling on the burrs at the base of the antler, I shouldn't have thought he was very old. Whatever his age, he must be an outstanding stag."

Baskerville laughed. "Well, he won't be outstanding for long. I want that stag, Platt. See if you can find him for us, and come the end of the summer I'll have his head for a hat rack."

Again Dick hesitated. He knew he was asking for trouble, but, he reflected ruefully, he might as well be hung for a sheep as for a lamb. "I'd be inclined to leave him alone, at least for a year or two," he ventured.

"Leave him alone," echoed Baskerville scornfully. "What sort of old woman's talk is this? I thought we hunted stags."

Dick sighed. Now he was really committed. He took a deep breath. "For some time now I've felt that the antler formation on a lot of the stags we've killed has left something to be desired. There are a lot of young stags, and stags with poor heads, being left to breed, and stags with poor heads breed poor youngsters. A few stags like this one would soon leave their impression on the herds, and in a few years' time we would see the benefit from them. Unless we become a lot more selective in culling than we are now, we are going to see a progressive degeneration in our stocks. Already, in Scotland, selective shooting is beginning to produce some fine heads. The stags may not be as heavy as ours, but the antler growth is there. Down here it almost seems as if we are hunting and killing the best stags and leaving the runts to breed."

Throughout Dick's speech, Baskerville listened in silence, his face darkening as he fought to stem the rage that welled inside him. Almost before Dick had finished speaking, he turned his heel and strode away, only to turn and come stalking back. He stood for a long moment staring at Dick, and the huntsman waited for the storm to break. Platt and the kennelman waited too. They wouldn't have left for all the stags on Exmoor.

At last Baskerville exploded. "Never," he exclaimed, "never in all my life have I had to stand and listen to such a load of unmitigated claptrap as I've just heard. How you can stand there, with the proof in your hand that Exmoor can still produce fine heads, and suggest that the deer are deteriorating baffles me. I cannot follow your reasoning. And as for leaving him to make his mark, well, unless I'm very much mistaken, he's made it already, last autumn."

He paused for breath, and took a pace or two up and down the concrete yard, but before anyone could speak he returned to the attack. "I'm a reasonable man, so I'll overlook the fact that you have chosen in public to make adverse criticism of the way in which I manage the affairs of the Hunt, unless," he added sarcastically, "you wish to go on record as being of the opinion that under my mastership the deer have deteriorated. Maybe you'd like to press for my resignation?"

Dick, utterly bewildered and astonished that Baskerville should have taken as a personal insult a suggestion made in all sincerity and innocence, and with the interests of stag hunting at heart, was too shaken to speak, but Baskerville had not finished yet. "What I will not tolerate, either here or anywhere else, from any member of the Hunt, is the slightest suggestion that stag hunting is not the best method of deer control on Exmoor. My conscience is quite clear on that score. There are no doubts in my mind. Stag hunting has been tried and tested for more than a century, and not found wanting. But then, I don't need to justify stag hunting, either to myself or anyone else. If you have any doubts in your mind, go and join this league, whatever it's called, the League for the Abolition of Blood Sports, or, if you're so impressed with the way things are run in Scotland, why not go there?"

Dick regarded the Master gravely. "I might just do that," was all he said.

"I don't care what you do," bellowed Baskerville, "but get out of my sight."

He strode away. Platt watched his retreating back and, when he was out of earshot, turned to Dick with a grin. "You fairly put the old man off his breakfast this morning," he said.

"Don't you agree with me?" asked Dick.

"What about?" asked Platt innocently.

"Why, about the quality of antler formation on Exmoor, of course," said Dick impatiently.

"You might be right," shrugged Platt, "but then, I'm only the harborer. When the day comes when I can't find a runnable stag, I'll agree with you."

"By then it will be too late," snapped Dick.

He brooded over the affair in the days that followed, and the more he thought about it, the more untenable his position seemed. He sincerely believed that it was the sacred duty of a sportsman to conserve his quarry and its environment, but to do this he must be prepared to adapt, to bend his ways to the changes that were taking place in the world. He did not feel he could retract his views, or change his beliefs and bow to the autocracy of the Hunt Master, yet he knew that he couldn't continue under the present state of affairs. During long sleepless nights he thought of the Scottish Highlands. He saw the wide lochs, and the mountains towering to the sky. He imagined the long stalk, the days alone on the hill, and at the end the clean shot, the quick kill, and the long trek home.

The old Exmoor was gone, vanishing in the maze of modern farming methods, and the old men were dying. Up in Scotland the land was still untamed, and the hills were wide and empty. A man might walk for a week and never come to a road.

At the end of a month he handed in his resignation. Baskerville never spoke to him again.

20

The Camp in the Sanctuary

The fine, warm spring dissolved into the wettest summer in living memory. Day followed day with the skies overcast and dull, with rain sweeping in silver cascades over the leaden landscape. The rivers ran at winter height, and the bogs on the moor were full.

Throughout July, Platt searched in vain for the great stag whose antler he had found earlier in the year. He rode for miles over the bare and windswept hills, the rain misting his binoculars and soaking him to the skin. He found a number of runnable stags, but never a thirteen, fourteen, or fifteen pointer. He realized that even if he did find such a stag there was no guarantee that it was the same individual, but he did not see that it mattered, as long as Baskerville got a head comparable to the antler he had seen. As the days went by, and his quarry continued to elude him, he began to wonder whether Dick had been right and that there was a general deterioration in deer stocks. Resolutely he put the thought from him. Somewhere there was such a stag. He had seen the evidence. All he had to do was find him.

Thoughout the rainy days Isaac also kept vigil, patrolling the oak woods at Slade Farm at odd intervals, keeping watch at dawn and dusk in case any poacher came near. He saw no sign of Rhus, but guessed that the big stag could well return in the rutting season. He saw no sign of poachers either. He had done his work well, and the sanctuary was left in peace.

Late one afternoon, as cloud misted the hills and rain fell in a fine drizzle, darkening the full-leaved oaks, Isaac walked slowly along the crest of the woods, looking down into the valley below. Suddenly he stopped, staring hard. Was it his imagination, a trick of light and mist, or could he see smoke? He watched carefully. Sure enough he saw it again, dense wreaths curling up among the oaks. Now he could smell it, and he moved purposefully downward, slipping silently through the trees, his great holly staff clutched in his hand.

When he reached the stream, his anxiety dissolved into mirth at the spectacle before him. Two youths had pitched camp beneath the oaks and were trying desperately to get a fire to burn. One knelt, his face aglow as he puffed at the sodden mess of sticks, while the other fanned frantically with a plate. Smoke rose in dense clouds, suffocating them and making them cough and splutter. Both boys were soaking wet, irritable, and out of temper.

Isaac decided it was time he took a hand, if ever they were going to get a meal that night. He stepped out of the shadow of the trees. "Troubled with mosquitoes, are you, lads?" he called.

Both boys started up, their expressions a mixture of anger and astonishment. Then the darker one grinned ruefully. "We're savoring the joys of an English summer. But at the moment it looks as though summer's winning. We are soaking wet, and starving, and we are fed up."

"Right then." Isaac laughed. "Let's see if I can help. If you've a mind to do as I say, you'll have a fire in ten minutes."

The two boys looked at each other and shrugged. "This I've got to see," said one. "Right, Daddy, we're in your hands. Tell us what to do."

"First of all, kick that lot away. You're trying to burn oak, and it's a sullen wood at the best of times." Swiftly he set them to gathering the paper-thin tendrils of dead bark that clung to the trunks of the birches by the stream. Next he showed them the needle-thin twigs which, although dead, were attached to the tree, but which broke with a snap when touched. When they collected enough, he led them to a grove of ash trees, and from the dead wood that littered the ground they gathered several armfuls.

Isaac laid the birch bark in a mound, away from the dripping trees, on the stones by the stream. He piled the twigs in conical fashion round the bark and applied a match. The smoky flames of the burning bark spluttered and leapt up to consume the twigs. Around the blaze he stacked twigs of slightly thicker diameter, gradually increasing the size of the sticks, and laying each one with care, so that air could circulate.

"Well done," said the younger boy. "You beat your deadline."

Isaac looked puzzled. "Deadline?" he queried.

"You said ten minutes," explained the boy. "You did it in nine and a half. I'd never have believed it if I hadn't seen it with my own eyes."

Half an hour later they sat round a roaring fire, the boys replete after a vast fry of bacon, eggs, beans, and tomatoes, Isaac drinking coffee out of a tin mug and enjoying himself hugely. Secretly, he was proud to have won the admiration of the boys, and he in turn found himself respecting the inner confidence that allowed the boys so readily to admit their weaknesses and mistakes. Perhaps there was hope for the world yet, he mused.

A sudden thought struck him. "I suppose you two have got permission from the owners to camp here?" he asked.

The boys looked at each other sheepishly. Then the dark-haired one spoke. "Not exactly. Let me introduce ourselves. I'm Tony Bakewell, and this here's Peter Bell. We're students from Bristol, and we're both members of the League for the Abolition of Blood Sports."

"Who own this land," commented Isaac.

"Exactly," nodded Tony. "We heard about this sanctuary, and we came here, expecting to find a warden, or somebody. We hoped to be able to help out in some way, restoring fences or something. When we got here and found it deserted we didn't know what to do, but since we were here we decided we couldn't do any harm spending the night here, especially since our money helped to buy the place. To tell the truth, we're bitterly disappointed with the setup, but we haven't had much time to discuss it yet. We've been too busy trying to survive. If it hadn't been for you, I expect we would still have been struggling."

He paused, leaning forward to throw fresh logs on the fire. "Come to think of it," he asked, "what are you doing here, wandering about like an overgrown boy scout?"

Isaac laughed. "I come and I go, and no one tries to stop me. But I too have worried about this farm, and if you like I'll tell you the story."

The two boys sat listening as Isaac told them the history of the place, starting with the story of Duncan Turner and ending with a description of how he put a stop to the poaching. When he had finished it was quite dark. The rain had stopped and stars glittered in the sky. The faces of the boys shone in the firelight, solemn and thoughtful.

"You're quite a character, aren't you?" said Tony.

"Round here they think I'm mad." Isaac chuckled.

"That figures," said Tony. "You're a sight too revolutionary in your ideas for them I fancy. But tell me. Forgive me for asking, but how could an old boy like you sort out a young poacher on your own?"

For answer Isaac picked the boy up, and held him,

kicking and struggling, high above his head, before setting him gently on his feet. "You've made your point," said Tony, bowing in mock servility. "In future kindly consider me on your side."

"This big stag?" asked Peter. "Is he safe now?"

Isaac shook his head. "He's nowhere near the sanctuary at present. At least, I've seen no sign of him. But his presence has been noted hereabouts, and I know the Hunt is interested in finding him, because the harborer was asking about him only the other day. Sooner or later they'll find him and hunt him down, unless he can get back in here, where the huntsmen dare not follow."

He clambered stiffly to his feet and stretched. "Now, boys, if you don't mind, it's getting late and I'm a long way from home. An old man like me needs his sleep."

"Will we see you again?" asked Peter.

"If you are still around, I might look in. At least you should be able to cook your breakfast tomorrow." He waved and moved off into the darkness. The two boys watched him go. A long while afterward they realized they did not know his name.

Sleep was slow in coming to them as they lay in the unfamiliar confines of their tent. The night was full of small alien sounds, the whisper of soft feet outside the camp, the short, dry cough of a sheep, and once, a thin, high scream that came from the hill, echoing in their minds and setting the hair on the back of their necks to creep. "Lord," groaned Tony, "if this is the peace and quiet of the countryside, give me the city any day."

"Quiet," hissed Peter. "Listen."

"That's the trouble," grumbled Tony. "I can't help listening. It's bedlam out there."

"There's someone out there," whispered Peter. "Someone or something. It's big, and it's getting nearer."

Tony lay still, and through the thin walls of the tent came the unmistakable sound of a heavy body being dragged through the undergrowth. For a moment it stopped, and then it came on, steadily drawing nearer. Tony fought to control the rising tide of fear that welled inside him. "I expect it's our old friend, bringing our morning's firewood or something."

Peter struggled out of his sleeping bag. "Whatever it is, I'm not going to be caught without my trousers," he muttered. "Come on."

Reluctantly, Tony followed, and clutching their flashlights, the two boys ventured out into the night. The thin beams of white light cut into the darkness, questing and wavering among the oaks. They could see nothing, but a heavy crashing away to their right sent Peter running through the wet bracken in the direction of the sound. Tony followed more cautiously, but the sight that met his eyes drove away fear and filled him with pity and hot anger.

A young hind lay on her side, her eyes rolling, her mouth open and her tongue hanging as she panted for breath. As the boys approached she lurched to her feet, to fall again and lie with distended, heaving flanks. Only then did they see the cause of her distress, a stout wire biting into the flesh of her hind leg and stretched taut to a heavy log. How far she had dragged her burden the

194

boys could only guess, but now, even though filled with fear at their presence, she could go no farther.

"The pliers," shouted Peter. "In the toolkit by the tent. And bring a blanket or something to throw over her head."

Obediently, Tony ran back to the camp. When he returned he found that Peter had wedged his flashlight in the fork of a tree, so that it shone on the stricken deer. Tony did the same, as Peter gently dropped the blanket over the hind's head. For a moment the hind lay still, but as soon as they laid hands on her she struggled so violently that the boys were flung into the undergrowth.

They tried again, this time flinging themselves on the hind so that their combined weight held her down, grasping the wet, slippery limbs and hanging grimly on until her struggles subsided. After that it was the work of a moment to cut the wire and pull it free from where it was embedded in the flesh. There was nothing they could do to treat the wound. They could only hope that it would heal naturally. They released the hind and took away the blanket that covered her head.

For a while the hind lay without moving, and the boys watched, fearful that they had caused her serious injury in struggling with her. Then suddenly she lurched to her feet, shook herself, and moved a few paces into the wood. To their astonishment she did not run away, but instead began to feed, browsing peacefully on the hazel bushes that hung low over her head. Gradually the undergrowth swallowed her up, and the wood was deserted once more.

Weary, wet and mud stained, the two boys returned

to the tent and crawled into their sleeping bags. "I think I know now why in olden days the punishments for deer poaching were so savage," remarked Tony. "Right now, if I could catch the man who set that snare, I'd gladly chop his hand off."

"I expect that was how our old friend felt when he caught his poacher," answered Peter. "It must have given him a certain satisfaction. Ironically, though, all he has succeeded in doing is to preserve the big stag for the attentions of the Hunt."

"Equally ironic is the fact that this so-called sanctuary is little more than a haunt for poachers," said Tony moodily. "Frankly, this whole business makes me sick."

"Would you be prepared to do something to stop stag hunting?" asked Peter suddenly, "or at least to draw public attention to the cruelty involved?"

"I'd certainly welcome suggestions a bit more positive than supporting a sanctuary that exists only in name, or just talking about the problem," said Tony.

"Then how's this for an idea? If, when we get back to college, we can get some of the other students interested, we can attend a meeting of the Hunt and stage a protest. Then, with a bit of luck, we can be in at the kill and try and save the stag. We may not succeed, but at least we'll attract attention, and maybe get public sympathy on our side. Then perhaps parliament will legislate against stag hunting."

Tony thought for a moment. "It's worth a try," he agreed. "We may not get very far, and I doubt if we will stop the Hunt, but as you say we might be able to arouse the apathetic public. I'm game."

"It's raining again," groaned Peter. "If this weather keeps up, we might just as well head back to town and start planning our campaign straightaway. We'll get nothing here except rheumatism and pneumonia."

There was silence in the tent, as the boys lay listening to the rain on the canvas. Soon its patter lulled them, and before long they slept.

21

The Hunt Saboteurs

The wet weather, which had so effectively ruined the boys' camping holiday, continued on into August. The hay harvest was ruined, and now the grain was rotting in the fields. Grim-faced farmers talked in the marketplace of hardships yet to come, and cattle sickened in the waterlogged pastures, their livers infested with the parasites that alone prospered in the damp.

The morning of the opening meet of the Severn Seas Hunt dawned fretful and gray, with clouds hanging in dark veils over the moorland hills. Mist obscured the landscape, and clung shimmering to every twig and leaf, every grass blade and sprig of heather. Platt rode slowly over the moor, his pony's hoofbeats muffled on the sodden turf, his mind occupied with nothing more than thoughts of breakfast. He had successfully harbored a stag for the Hunt, but so far his search for the giant stag so coveted by Baskerville had been a complete failure.

His way down to the road, and the farm where the meet was to be held, was blocked by a narrow combe. For a moment he was tempted to cut straight across, but consideration for his pony, and the thought that he would have to lead it up the side of the combe, made slippery and treacherous by the heavy rains, prompted him to make a longish detour, skirting the edge of the valley.

Sheer force of habit made him glance down into the combe as he rode. The trees were in full leaf, a dark shielding canopy that obscured all visibility, but here and there the trees thinned, revealing small glades, thickly carpeted with tall fern. A patch of dull red quickened his interest. Was it simply a frond of dying fern? It looked too solid and dense. A solitary hind no doubt, or perhaps one of a herd that lay completely concealed, sheltering from the weather.

Then Platt saw the antler, and his heart missed a beat as he reined in his pony. Dismounting, he took his binoculars from their case and focused them carefully. A moment's inspection left him in no doubt. The stag's head was hidden, but the thickness of the neck, and the spreading sweep of the massive branching horn, told him that here was the prize he had searched for all summer. He had found the big stag, not by the sea or in the deer sanctuary, but right under his feet, and not a mile from where the Hunt was due to meet. For a while he watched, fearful lest the stag should decide to move. Only when he was certain that it had settled for the day did he move quietly away, but it was a long time before his heart ceased its hammering.

By nine o'clock the skies had cleared. A cold wind tempered the heat of the sun and drove ragged white clouds racing across the blue bowl of the sky. Baskerville was not deceived. He knew that by nightfall it would be raining again, and that throughout the day the going would be rough on horse and rider alike, the ground soft and treacherous, the bogs as full as at any time in the winter. He dressed with his usual care, but as he donned the red jacket, the hunting pink of time-honored tradition, he wondered ruefully what sort of mud-spattered spectacle he would present by evening.

In company with his groom, who led the second horse he would ride that day, he set off on the short journey to the meet. High beech hedges bordered the lane, their branches almost meeting overhead, and the morning was full of the silence of high summer. Only the soft clop of the horses' hooves, the creak of leather, and the faint jingling of harness broke the stillness. Baskerville felt a great wave of contentment mingle with the undercurrent of anticipation and excitement as he thought of what the day might bring.

Startled and irritated, he heard the drum of hooves as someone came galloping along the lane toward them. "What idiot can be riding a horse like that over a hard surface?" he exclaimed. "Does he want to cripple his mount for life?"

Next moment the rider appeared round the bend of the lane, and to Baskerville's surprise he saw that it was Ted Sheratt, the last person, he would have thought, to misuse his mount, or to behave in so reckless a fashion. Ted reined to a halt, and raised his cap in greeting. "I came as fast as I dared, Master. I felt you ought to be warned at once. There could be trouble at the meet."

"What sort of trouble?" asked Baskerville quietly.

"There's several carloads of young people, students I'd say, no one from these parts. They've come apparently to protest against our hunting. They've got banners and placards."

"Is there any fighting?" asked Baskerville quickly.

"Not yet," replied Ted. "They're just standing quietly, in a line outside the farm gate, but some of the Hunt followers are angry and shouting for them to go home."

Baskerville turned to his groom. "Ride back quickly. Telephone the county police and ask for Superintendent Peterson. My compliments, and I fear a breach of the peace is likely to occur at the meet. I'd be grateful for a strong motorcycle patrol with all speed."

The groom wheeled his horse and cantered away. Baskerville rode steadily on to the meet, Ted following and leading the spare horse.

A derisive cheer greeted their arrival at the farm gate. Baskerville rode slowly along the line of students, his face a mask, his only acknowledgment of their presence a brief raising of his whip to touch his cap. Nothing in his expression or demeanor betrayed his anger or disgust as he surveyed them. Was this, he wondered, the sort of freedom in support of which he had risked his life in two world wars? Had the virtues of democracy and free speech degenerated into a form of chimps' tea party, loud with senseless screams of defiance and hate?

The hair of some of the boys was so long that it was difficult to tell them from the girls, and it was no good going by their dress. Garish, cheap shirts, faded blue jeans, and shabby, inadequate footwear seemed to be the uniform of them all. Some of the girls wore no shoes at all. What were their parents thinking of, he wondered, allowing them so much freedom, when they displayed so little sense?

He read the banners and placards as he passed them by. BAN HUNTING, SAVE OUR STAGS, HUNTING IS OBSCENE, THOU SHALT NOT KILL. They'll stop at nothing, Baskerville thought, not even blasphemy. And this was the generation that was to inherit the earth.

He rode into the farmyard and turned to face the crowd, waiting until there was silence. Then he spoke. "As I have often said in the past, this is a free country, and anyone is entitled to come here, ask questions, express his opinions, and make whatever comment or protest he thinks fit. But we are a law-abiding community, going about our lawful business. I intend to keep it that way, and what is more, I intend that this meeting shall proceed according to custom. I would remind our visitors that this yard is private property, and to encroach upon it would be an act of trespass. You are welcome to remain where you are, but you must not obstruct the entrance."

A ragged burst of applause from the Hunt followers greeted this speech, echoed by jeers from the protesters. Tony detached himself from the group of students and walked to the gate. "I have no questions to ask," he said in a loud voice, "nor do I intend to trespass. We are here to protest against the vile and barbaric custom of stag hunting. We are here to condemn the unnecessary slaughter of innocent animals. We beg everyone of you to ask yourselves whether you wish to be a party to this practice. There will come a time when stag hunting will be banned by law. If you wish to win our respect and confidence, stop it now. Give it up of your own accord."

As Tony finished speaking Baskerville rode forward to the gate. Wheeling his mount so that he was broadside on to the boy, he leaned over in the saddle. "Go home, son," he said curtly. "Get your hair cut, and then perhaps you'll be able to see things more clearly."

Tony swung round to face the students. "Did you hear that?" he yelled. "Isn't it typical?" He turned back to Baskerville. "Unlike you, sir, who regards everyone under twenty-five as a sex-mad, drug-swilling degenerate, we know you for what you are, one of a small, sadistic minority in an otherwise decent generation, selfish enough to want to go your own way regardless of the effect on other people. What is more, you encourage women and children to witness your brutalities."

Baskerville said nothing. He had regretted the remark about the haircut the instant it had passed his lips. Now he felt that the less he said the better. He stole a quick glance at his watch. If he was to keep to his timetable, the tufters should move off in ten minutes. He doubted very much if the police would arrive on time, but not for a moment did he consider altering his routine.

Tony was addressing the students again, his voice loud enough for all to hear. "In an hour or two, this 'law-abiding community' will kill a stag in broad daylight. This at a time of year when the whole district is thronged with holidaymakers, men, women, and children, from towns and cities. What sort of introduction is this to country life, to be an unwilling spectator at a public execution, to watch a stag bleed to death while the hounds fight over his entrails?"

"You're talking nonsense," snapped Baskerville. "The stag is always humanely destroyed before hounds are allowed near."

"Always?" shouted Tony.

"Always," retorted Baskerville. He beckoned to Platt, who had been waiting all the while, almost bursting in his eagerness to give the Master his news. To Tony he said, "We've heard your protest, and given you the chance to express your opinions. You cannot say we haven't been fair. Now we must proceed with the day's sport."

"Sport?" yelled Tony. "Butchery you mean. Don't forget to be fair to the stag, slaughterman."

Ignoring him, Baskerville rode to meet Platt. He had to lean forward in his saddle to hear the harborer's excited whisper. "I've found him, sir. The big one. He lies in Winney Combe, not a mile distant."

Baskerville said nothing, but his slow smile of satisfaction told Platt all he wanted to know. Tufters were drawn from the cattle truck parked in the yard, and as they danced excitedly among the hooves of the waiting horses, the slow minutes crawled by, until they reached the stroke of eleven. At a sign from Baskerville the Hunt moved off, between the ranks of the protesters.

Then it happened. The hounds had almost passed the line of students when from out of their ranks flew a white canister that burst in a pale yellow cloud as it fell among the tufters. Two of the hounds went down, screaming in pain as they writhed on the ground and tried to claw the stinging pepper from their nostrils and eyes. The others scattered, yelping and sneezing as they inhaled the dust. A huntsman spurred forward, swinging his long whip, only to have a placard broken over his head. The horse bolted, its haunch gashed and bleeding from the broken end of the stick to which the placard had been nailed.

Tony Bakewell gasped in anger and dismay. "Who did that?" he shouted to Peter. "We agreed there was to be no disturbance."

Peter shook his head in bewilderment. "I don't know. It must be that group who joined us at the last moment. They'll land us all in . . ."

His words were lost as the Hunt streamed out of the farmyard, to be greeted by a shower of soot and flour bombs. Within minutes individual fights had broken out, both on the road and in the yard, as Hunt followers grappled with students, and the protesters, innocent and guilty alike, strove to defend themselves. Grimly, implacably, Baskerville rode off, with the Hunt following.

Behind them the battle raged on. Tony and Peter stood helpless, taking no part in the fighting and stand-

ing well to one side. Arthur Feather, never one to miss an opportunity like this, flung his arms around a buxom young girl. She screamed, and suddenly Arthur was seized from all sides and borne aloft. In the corner of the yard was a large manure heap, moist and redolent with the rains of the summer. In a moment Arthur was flying through the air, to sink deep into the middle of the squelching mass. Cursing and screaming, he struggled to extricate himself, only to be thrust back into the mire.

The high-pitched roar of motorcycle engines woke Peter to urgent action. "Come on," he yelled, tugging at Tony's arm. "It's the police. They'll arrest us all."

Tony hesitated. "Why should I run? I've done nothing wrong."

"Do you think they'll believe that?" shouted Peter. "You're the ringleader. They'll blame the whole thing on you. Come on, run, while you've got the chance. Follow me."

He disappeared behind a barn, and Tony followed, a few moments before the police motorcycles, followed by a Land-Rover, roared into the yard. Arthur Feather staggered from the manure heap, covered with dung and dirty straw, waving his arms and shouting hysterically, "I know them, officer. I'll make a statement. I charge them all with assault."

The sergeant in charge of the police squad turned a bleak eye on the apparition. "When I want a statement from you, Sweet William," he remarked coldly, "I'll take one. Meantime, you're under arrest, charged with making an affray along with the others. Now get in line."

Aghast, and speechless with rage, Arthur did as he was told. Bitterly, he reflected that everyone present had heard the sergeant call him Sweet William. Never again in his life, he knew, would he be known as anything else.

Half a mile away, Tony and Peter plunged through a canopy of tall fern and into a small wood, where they collapsed, panting, on the ground. "What now?" gasped Tony.

"Lie low," said Peter. "Even if anyone's missed us, they won't bother to search. They haven't a hope of finding us, and our lot won't give us away. We'll hide here until dark, and then hitch a lift back to Bristol. What a good job we didn't come in our own car."

"We're going to be pretty hungry by nightfall," grumbled Tony. "Ah well, at least it isn't raining."

"Are you sure?" chuckled Peter.

Tony lifted his face to the breeze, and groaned as he felt the cool caress of the fine rain.

They passed an anxious as well as an uncomfortable day. For a long time they could hear the distant clamor of the hounds, and once they heard the thunder of horses' hooves. Late that night, soaking wet and famished, they staggered into a diner on the main road to Bristol, where a friendly truck driver offered them a lift.

He asked no questions. His truck was fitted with a radio, and he had heard an account of the day's events on the local news. He guessed what they had been up to, but said nothing. A staunch Socialist, and a city man, he was on their side.

22

The Last Run

Baskerville waited by the side of the combe, his brow
dark, his whole appearance so grim and forbidding that
no one dared approach him. Three hours had passed, and
so far the tufters had drawn a blank. The original pack
had been replaced by fresh hounds; three hinds and a
young stag had been flushed from the combe, but of the
big stag there had been not a sign.

The field had thinned considerably. Half the meet had
gone home, either to change their soot-stained garments,
or simply because they had wearied of waiting. Baskerville stayed on, although his clothes were ruined and the
smell of soot was rank and nauseating in his nostrils. To

make matters worse, the skies had darkened, and a thin rain had started to fall, turning the flour and soot into a thin, glutinous paste that defied all efforts to remove it. An hour ago, Baskerville had curtly refused a request from Platt that they should draw the wood where the other stag was harbored. Now he regretted his decision, but steadfastly refused to alter it.

Rhus lay hidden in the combe. At one point the stream fell away in a short waterslide and poured into a long, narrow pool. On one side of the pool the bank was high and steep, but on the other side it was low, with lank ferns hanging down to trail in the water. Rhus lay under the bank, in a low cave less than three feet high. Here the water was deep, and so Rhus was able to stand upright, completely concealed. To find him a man would have to crawl upstream on hands and knees.

A young hound limped through the wood. He was weary and exhausted, all enthusiasm for the chase spent in the first hour of roistering through the combe. Now he crawled down to the stream, just below where Rhus lay hidden, and lapped gratefully at the cool water. The scent of Rhus was faint, but a slight whiff reached the hound's nostrils. Immediately he gave tongue.

Far away in the woods the huntsman cocked an ear to the sound. He was new to the district, having replaced the young man Dick, who had left earlier in the summer. He was acutely aware that he was on trial in the neighborhood and deeply chagrined that this first test had been such a bitter failure. He listened again, and now he was sure that the hound giving tongue was young Wrestler. He had chosen him in spite of his youth and inexperience because he had noticed that he was an unusually silent hound, only giving voice when necessary. Suddenly hopeful, he called in the rest of the hounds and rode in the direction of the sound.

His heart sank when he arrived at the scene, to find Wrestler baying at an apparently empty pool, but at that moment a dipper flew upstream and into the ferns that overhung the bank. Next moment it was out, flying on with a piping call of alarm, and the huntsman urged his hounds into the water.

It was stalemate. Hounds found and circled the hidden stag, and Rhus stood at bay before he had even been roused. For a moment the huntsman was in a state bordering on panic. Already he could hear the clattering of hooves as other riders came to join him. Strictly speaking, the etiquette of the Hunt demanded that the stag be taken at once, but although the new huntsman had no idea how Baskerville would react in such a situation, he felt sure that if the stag was killed without a run, particularly at the opening meet, he would not be too popular with either the Master or the field. Throwing caution to the wind, he dismounted and plunged into the pool.

Rhus exploded from cover in a fountain of spray, hounds clamored, and for Wrestler, his brief moment of fame ended in a choking scream, as Rhus impaled him on his antlers and flung him far into the undergrowth. Then water flew in fine spurts from the bed of the stream, as Rhus bounded away. A few minutes later the huntsman was reporting to the Master that the stag had been roused, and the Hunt was afoot.

Still Rhus was reluctant to leave the combe, and for another hour they hunted him up and down the stream, sometimes losing him for minutes at a time. Hounds could not follow the trail as long as Rhus stayed in the stream, for the water left no scent, but always the huntsmen came to their aid, finding water splashes and bruised ferns that marked the passage of their quarry through the woods. At last they drove him out of the combe, and up on to the moors.

So began a chase that was to be remembered by those who took part in it as one of the most grueling and exhausting of all times. Rhus led them in a wide circle, often lost in the rain and the fog, with hounds following, strung out in a long line, toiling up the heather-clad slopes, crossing the quaking bogs of the grassy uplands, plunging into steep and ferny combes, or slipping stealthily along beech-fringed lanes.

The hours passed, and gradually the field thinned as riders gave up the chase. One by one they dropped out, some thrown and floundering in the moorland bogs, some with mounts lame and exhausted by the long run. Others simply fell so far behind that they had no means of finding which way the rest had gone.

At first Rhus ran easily, breasting the tall fern and thrusting through the thickets of thorn that barred his way. At times he left the Hunt so far behind that he was able to rest and cool his aching limbs in the black water of a peat bog or the clear pools of the moorland streams, but gradually the baying pack began to press closer, and though he ran steadily, seemingly possessed of an inexhaustible strength, the pace began to tell.

As evening came he ran for the sea. Only three riders were left in the field, and Baskerville was one of them. He had ridden one horse to a standstill, and now his second mount was so tired that at times it stumbled and almost fell, threatening to unseat him and throw him to the ground. As the wooded cliffs that bordered the Severn sea came into view below him, Baskerville was just in time to see his quarry vanish among the trees, the baying pack hard on his heels. Baskerville drove his horse downward, exulting in the triumphant thought that any moment now, the stag would stand at bay, the tall cliffs a barrier beween him and the sea.

Rhus crashed through the dense, spindly woodland, his hooves slipping on the wet, crumbly soil as he ran aslant the slope of the hill. Baskerville heard the wild clamor of the hounds, and guessing which line the stag had taken, he shouted with pleasure. He knew the woods well, had played in them as a boy, and he knew of a wide track which led along the cliff edge and which would carry him straight to where, any moment now, the stag would stand at bay.

Many years ago, on a stormy night in November, as the moon hid behind racing clouds, a vole had scampered over the cliff face, an ash seed in its tiny jaws. For a long second, the treacherous moon revealed the presence of the vole to a hunting owl, and the vole died, the seed falling from its grasping jaws. The seed lodged behind a rock, a massive sandstone slab, and from the seed sprouted a shoot. For a while the tree flourished, until a gale tore it up by the roots, and tumbled it down into the tide, leaving a gaping hole in the cliff. Then the slow and inexorable forces of erosion got to work, and as the years ticked by, second by second, the wind and the rain, the hot sun, and stinging frost weakened the cliff face more and more. Then came the wettest summer in living memory.

Thus from such small events, the death of a vole, the loss of a seed, the destinies of men are shaped, and time, the grim jester, ordains our fates before we are even born. Baskerville did not, could not, know that only the previous evening the cliff face had crumbled and fallen away. At an easy canter he rose his horse round a bend in the track. Then, instead of the broad green track he had known all his life, there was only the red raw scar of the broken cliff face, and beneath him, a yawning chasm that dropped sheer away to the beach below.

Cursing, he strove to halt his terrified mount. The horse screamed and reared, its hind legs slipping on the treacherous earth. Then it plunged forward, and Baskerville fell four hundred feet onto the rocks. For a while there came a steady rattle of loose stones from the cliff, and then there was only the endless chatter of small waves breaking on the shore.

Rhus ran on, skirting the edge of the landslide and plunging down the precipitous cliffs, sliding over patches of loose shale and leaping from rock to rock. Tangled clumps of gorse and long tussocky grass held for a brief instant before crumbling beneath his weight. A dozen times at least it seemed he must slip and fall to his death on the rocks below, but somehow, miraculously, he reached the shore, and by the time a scattered knot of hounds had gained the beach, he was swimming far out to sea. For a long while his antlers showed above the waves. Hounds followed him, but gradually the mist and darkness swallowed him up. Defeated, spiritless, the hounds turned and crawled back to shore.

Rhus swam in a wide circle. It was quite dark when at last he regained the beach, and climbed out onto the stones, several miles down the coast. Shaking himself free of the salt spray, he climbed stiffly up into the woods.

They buried Baskerville in the small churchyard that lay below the brow of the hill, and to Isaac it seemed that the whole neighborhood had come to attend the funeral. Down the narrow lane, behind the hearse that carried the coffin, they followed by the hundreds, in cars and on foot, some even on the sturdy Exmoor ponies they preferred to any other form of transport. They filled the tiny church and overflowed into the graveyard, where they stood bareheaded in the sun-drenched silence of the summer afternoon.

Isaac stood near the open grave, brooding as the earth was cast on to the coffin. The priest intoned the order for the burial of the dead, and Isaac listened to the familiar phrases, "We therefore commit his body to the ground, ashes to ashes . . ."

The plaintive mewing of a buzzard, wheeling high in the blue vault of the sky, fell on Isaac's ears, and involuntarily he glanced upward. As his gaze swept the crest of the hill he thought for a moment he saw a lone stag, his antlers arched like the spreading branches of a great oak, his hide red in the sun. When he looked again the stag had gone, and only the somber oaks stood dark against the sky.

Yet Isaac was certain his eyes had not deceived him, and the appearance of the stag had seemed to him at once a reassurance and a warning. After the funeral he walked alone, up through the leafy trees and out onto the bare shoulder of the hill, where the grasses trembled in the breeze from the sea, and the ghosts of the bronze men whispered to the sky. Sitting there, it came to him then that greed and avarice, power and self-interest, were no more than names men gave to a built-in urge for self-destruction. It seemed to him then that if man could not destroy himself in any other way, he would succeed by destroying his entire world.

Yet even if the holocaust came, and whole civilizations crumbled and decayed, it might still be possible that some would remain, those who lived in harmony with their surroundings and in sympathy with the rest of the living world. Maybe the meek would inherit the earth. He would not live to see it, but it was a good thought to carry with him, wherever he might go.